Mrs. Richard S. Greenough

Treason at Home

A novel. Part 2

Mrs. Richard S. Greenough

Treason at Home
A novel. Part 2

ISBN/EAN: 9783337065461

Printed in Europe, USA, Canada, Australia, Japan

Cover: Foto ©Andreas Hilbeck / pixelio.de

More available books at **www.hansebooks.com**

TREASON AT HOME.

A NOVEL.

IN THREE VOLUMES.

BY

MRS. GREENOUGH.

VOL. II.

London:

T. CAUTLEY NEWBY, PUBLISHER
30, WELBECK STREET, CAVENDISH SQUARE,
1865.

TREASON AT HOME.

CHAPTER I.

FROM that day the division between the cousins grew rapidly wider. Each was wounded to the quick by the coldness and avoidance of the other, and each expressed that grief by increased distance of manner. Walter was seldom in the house, and hunted with renewed energy. Edith devoted herself assiduously to her drawing. All the little daily customs which had brought them into contact were laid aside. The game of chess in the evening was discontinued, and the afternoon walks were given up. They only met before others. At such times they exerted their utmost efforts to appear cheerful and unconcerned, succeeding so well as to completely blind Mrs. Arden to the real state of things before her eyes.

"It was not so very strange, to be sure," she said to herself, "that Walter, so fond of horses and dogs as he had always been, should go back to his usual amusements after a while. And Edith had always been in the habit of seeing a great deal of company ; it was natural that she should begin to want a little variety. What a nice thing it was that this ball was coming off!" So saying, Mrs. Arden began to lay plans for a little dance at the Hall, and some dinner parties for the young people.

Only on one point did her aunt interfere with Edith. After five days of abstinence from riding, she told her that she really couldn't consent to her giving it up, she really couldn't. She noticed that Edith had quite lost her appetite, and she was sure it was that; she must beg that Edith wouldn't insist on stopping her rides. It troubled her so much to see her sit without tasting anything. She'd ordered all sorts of dishes, and Edith did not so much as look at them, and when she had seen her that morning refuse those cream cup cakes, she felt that really something must be done about it; and since she could not take anything to keep her up, except open air and exercise, open air and exercise she must take. Whereupon, Edith, after a vain resistance, invited Isabel to join Walter and herself in their morning rides, an invitation which Isabel gladly accepted, by her gay chatter relieving the embarrassment resulting from the changed position of the other two members of the party.

This arrangement definitively confirmed Walter in the belief that Edith had detected the state of his feelings, and was determined to put a stop to them.

The long, miserable days dragged themselves on, and the night of the ball arrived.

Mr. Arden had sent down on the preceding day a large box and an écrin, which severally contained a ball-dress of tulle and white heath, and a set of pearls.

"Oh, I can't wear them, they are much too handsome," Edith exclaimed, as her aunt opened the case, and displayed the pear-shaped ornaments.

"But, my dear, you know if your father sent them he expects you to wear them, and you ought, you know ; indeed, I really think you ought," rejoined Mrs. Arden, inspecting the large, lustrous drops.

"I wish he had sent something simpler; but if he wishes it I suppose I must," Edith replied, submissively.

In all her life Edith had never disobeyed her father, never disregarded a desire he had expressed. That instinctive obedience to parents which forms the first development of the religious sentiment, in her was peculiarly strong. Her father's wishes were her laws, in small as well as in great things. Accordingly, to Nitson's rapturous delight, both ball-dress and pearls were to be worn.

As Edith, wrapped in her cloak of white satin and lämmergeier, descended to the drawing-room on the night of the ball, she found Walter standing with a bouquet of carefully chosen flowers in his hand. His eyes glanced rapidly over her draped figure and rested on the bunch of tea roses, sent by Isabel, which she held.

"So you've got a bouquet already. I hoped you would wear these," he said, in a constrained tone.

Edith might have told him that a yard of white satin ribbon enabled a young lady to wear two bouquets at a time; but while she was confusedly uttering her thanks and trying to find words to explain the possibility, Walter cast the flowers carelessly upon the table and turned aside. Mrs. Arden came forward.

"Well, then, my dear, if you are quite ready."

Two carriages were waiting without.

"Two carriages. Why, what is that for?" Mrs. Arden exclaimed.

"I ordered the other for myself, aunt. I

thought I should make one too many in yours.
Ladies' dresses won't bear squeezing. May I ask
you for the first quadrille?" he added, to Edith,
a little hurriedly, handing her into the carriage.
"I must secure it now, or give it up altogether."

Edith said yes, the carriage door was shut, and
they took the road to the Park.

The night was black and still. Not a breath
stirred the frosty air; no stars were out. Impenetrable gloom enveloped every object outside
the narrow circle lighted by the carriage lamps,
Edith leaned back in silence.

"— do you, my dear?" caught her ear after a
while.

"I beg your pardon—what was it?"

"I was saying, my dear, that the Park must
be crowded, isn't it?"

"Yes, quite so. Isabel has given up her own
room."

"Dear me, given up her own room. Why, she
means to sleep somewhere, doesn't she?"

"Yes ; but all the rooms were taken up except

Lady Anne's bed-chamber, and they did not want to put any stranger there, of course. So she has taken it. She says she would like to see a ghost."

" She'll get well frightened some day if she isn't careful," responded Mrs. Arden. " People don't know what they are talking about when they jest on ghosts. But here we are," she added, interrupting herself, as the carriage turned into the gates of the park.

Great torches were planted in the ground before the sphinxes. The light glared fitfully, casting strange shadows over their stony faces. Their eyeballs seemed to move, their lips looked ready to unclose, as the red blaze rose and fell beneath them. Along the file of pines which lined the avenue were suspended coloured lamps, which threw strange and unnatural tints in rapid alternation upon the guests as they drove by. The sound of gay music reached them as they neared the house.

The ancient saloon, usually so sombre, was

now blazing with light. The waxed panels reflected like mirrors the hundred wax candles. A painting of Judith bearing the head of Holofernes hung opposite the door. The Jewish widow's eyes were cast as if fixed on the mistress of the house, who had taken her stand directly before her.

As Edith approached Lady Tremyss, she raised her eyes, which she had lowered at the sound of the whisper that greeted her entrance. She half drew back. Robed in the costliest lace, a diadem of antique cameos set in brilliants blazing on her forehead, her neck and arms flashing back the light, her eyes contradicting with their ominous lustre the marble stillness of the rest of her face, Lady Tremyss impressed Edith as something terrible—, beautiful, but with the blood-chilling beauty of a Medusa.

Beside Lady Tremyss stood Isabel, with her gay and sparkling face, her rose-coloured dress and wreath. While Edith was murmuring her words of acknowledgment in reply to Lady Tremyss' greeting, Isabel caught her hand.

"How sweetly you are dressed, and what splendid pearls those are; only you are looking as pale as a pearl yourself. You are not tired already, I hope?"

"No."

"And you have worn my bouquet. That is good in you. I was afraid that Walter would give you a handsomer, and that you would leave mine at home."

Isabel's attention was here claimed by some new arrivals, and Edith was glad to be able to turn away. As she drew back, Mr. Tracey took his place beside her, and she saw young Renson advancing, crush hat in hand.

"I am delighted to meet you, delighted to see the Park thrown open again. Fine house, though the rooms are rather low, very fine," said the old gentleman.

"This is the first time for several years, I believe," said Edith.

"Yes; not since the death of Sir Ralph. A trying evening for Lady Tremyss it must be;

and, indeed, there is something about her rather
different from usual, it seems to me," remarked
Mr. Tracey, looking at his hostess.

"I think I never saw her look so handsome
before," replied Edith, who did not care to con-
fess the impression produced upon her by Isabel's
mother.

"Perhaps so; but that is not what I meant,"
responded Mr. Tracey; then lowering his voice,
he added, as if impelled by a sudden impulse,
"Do you know, I can't imagine a man's being
in love with that woman; and as to marrying
her, I'd as lief marry that Lamy—Lama—you
know some one wrote a poem about her—"

"Lamia," suggested Edith, assisted to her
conclusion rather by the probabilities of the case,
than by any aid afforded by Mr. Tracey's recollec-
tions.

"Yes—a Lamia, out right."

Mr. Tracey's remarks were interrupted by the
appearance of young Renson, looking rather
redder and stiffer than usual. Mr. Renson did

not waltz; he engaged Edith for the second quadrille. He was closely followed by Lady Emily Marsh, who presented her nephew, Mr. George Osborne, a tall, cadaverous youth, with stiff black hair, a sparse moustache, and an eye-glass, who requested the first waltz.

"I never dance quadrilles, they are so stiff and solemn," he continued, in a patronising manner. "There is something petrifying in all those right angles. Don't you think so?"

"The angular, the stiff, and the solemn. Yes, taken together, they are oppressive, I acknow-ledge."

There was a faint smile hovering about her mouth that rather perplexed Mr. Osborne, but he had no time to deliberate. Isabel came up at that instant and spoke to Edith.

"I am to dance the first dance with Lord Skeffington, and the second with Walter. You'll be my vis-à-vis, won't you?"

Edith assented.

"You're engaged to Walter, of course, and after that?"

"To Mr. Renson, and Mr. Osborne."

"Half-a-dozen men have been begging introductions, but I've put them off until after the quadrille. Walter,"—to young Arden, who just then came up—"you are to be my vis-à-vis."

Walter offered Edith his arm, and they followed Isabel into the dancing-room. It was, as Isabel had said it should be, filled with flowers. Opposite the entrance was a large mirror, before which stood two gigantic vases of oriental porcelain, supporting pyramids of flowers.

"See, are they not superb?" said Isabel, directing Edith's attention to them. "They are a present from your father He sent them down, flowers and all, with a man to take care of them. They arrived this afternoon. Such a great packing box as it was! Aren't they magnificent?"

"I suppose they are, since papa chose them. They are very fashionable, I know," replied

Edith. " But you said there were no mirrors in this room."

" Oh, yes, Mamma had that one put there to please me, and it is very nice, after all."

Edith had supposed that she would be painfully observant of Walter's every look and motion ; but it was not so.   She felt giddy and bewildered. She had never seen him at a party before.   It seemed to make a stranger of him, and he seemed to feel the same thing with regard to her.

During the ten minutes, after the quadrille, Edith promised dances to half the men in the room, including Lord Skeffington. A momentary opening in the circle around her was immediately filled up by Mr. George Osborne, who had recovered his equanimity.

"A very pretty ball, really," he said, glancing about him as if he had not expected it to be pretty at all. " I am rather glad on the whole that I came. My aunt begged so that I couldn't refuse. Balls are great bores in general, don't you think so ? " looking superciliously around.

" One is exposed to meeting great bores at them, I acknowledge."

"Ah, that is where we men have the advantage of you ladies. You have to stand still, and smile, and say yes and no, while we can go off, and cut the annoyance. I never remain a half minute near a bore."

" Indeed," said Edith, glancing at him through her lashes, " I should have fancied that would have been more difficult. I have heard of persons condemned to pass their lives in the company of a bore ; they could no more escape from his presence than they could from themselves."

" Confoundedly stupid they must have been," rejoined Mr. Osborne, with an air of sovereign contempt.

The prelude to the waltz interrupted the conversation. Mr. Osborne prided himself upon his waltzing, though why he should do so it was difficult to discover. Edith did not share his opinion, and after two or three rounds, sat down, preferring his conversation to his dancing.

"Ah, you're easily fatigued, I see," said her partner, in a disappointed tone. "As for me, I am never tired. I could waltz all night."

"Alone," Edith suggested.

"No, not alone, of course not," he replied, a little piqued. "There's no need of waltzing alone, when so few men know what good waltzing is," he added, drawing himself up with an air of complacency; then putting his eye-glass in his eye, he surveyed the room.

"It's surprising what dull faces one meets at such places. Look at that heavy, middle-aged man in the door-way. Is he not enough to put a whole room to sleep?"

"Ah, I see, Mr. Watcherlie. Would you be so kind as to give your opinion of him? I see you quite pique yourself upon your skill in physiognomy," replied Edith, treacherously.

"Ah, well—yes, I do consider myself a little strong there."

Mr. Osborne twisted his moustache, and

studied the heavy, middle-aged man in the doorway.

"I am sorry not to have a better specimen to take in hand," he said, after a moment. "There are no salient points to take hold of. A good natured, rather stupid man, quite a clod-hopper—intellectually speaking, you know. One of those men who come into the world expressly to eat good dinners, and who care for nothing else."

"Really, you quite surprise me," said Edith, looking at the unconscious subject of Mr. Osborne's remarks. "I had no idea he was that sort of man."

"Ah, yes—it's a great study, physiognomy," replied Mr. Osborne complacently. "Who did you say he was?"

"Mr. Watcherlie, of Kinbourne Castle ; the anonymous author of ' Babel Revisited,' " returned Edith demurely.

Mr. Osborne's countenance fell. He dropped his eye-glass, stooped to pick it up, elbowed a plump lady in rising, and took advantage of Mr.

Renson's appearance to claim the second quadrille, to effect his retreat.

The evening wore on, as all evenings will. Edith's partners talked a great deal to her, but did not seem to require any particular conversational exertion on her part. They all said the same things. How long she had been there? whether she liked it? whether she did not find it dull after Arden Court? whether she intended to stay long? The last question went through her like a stab at each recurrence.—How long was she to stay? Did she wish to stay? But how could she bear to go away?—And her eye wandered in quest of Walter where he stood talking to other women.

At last the longed-for moment came. Walter led her into the circle of dancers, passed his arm around her and bore her round. The music, the odour of the flowers, the lights, Edith's beauty, that evening more peculiar and remarkable than ever, had roused young Arden's emotions almost beyond his control.

There was a fierce, reckless look about him that half terrified Edith when, on stopping, she stole a glance at his face.

"I had no idea you danced so well," he said abruptly. "It's a pity I did not profit by it last summer. You would have waltzed with me then the hour together."

Edith flushed violently.

Walter went on—"But now you are Miss Arden, I must take my turn with the rest. Curse me if I do, though; I'll never waltz with you again." —Could this be Walter—so rude, so ungentlemanly? What could it all mean?—She would have felt angry with him once, but she felt no anger now. The look he gave her as he spoke—that fierce, hungry, imploring look, prevented all such possibility.

"Bring Edith into the supper-room; I am going to have an ice," said Isabel, passing them.

Walter led Edith into the supper-room, and found her a chair. Isabel came up.

" Walter, you have danced her to death. You

never stopped. Now, Edith, do you stay here quietly and rest. I won't let any one speak to you."

Isabel posted herself as a sentinel before Edith, after obtaining a promise that she would try to eat the ice Walter had gone to bring. He brought it, and gave it to her without a word.

Edith felt a choking sensation in her throat —Oh, that would not do. She must think of something else.—At that moment Walter was called away.

She looked up. The supper-room was comparatively deserted, the view to the dancing-room was open; through the door she saw a crowd of gauzy dresses, white, pink, and blue, intermingled with deep toned brocades, ponderous velvets, laces, diamonds, plumes, black coats and white cravats, all under a blaze of light. It seemed very far off, and yet a moment ago she had been there, waltzing with Walter. As she gazed wistfully, a tall figure, taller than any in the crowded room beyond, passed before her. She started violently.   It was Goliath, dark, silent, sinister. She turned her head away, and saw two old gentlemen standing by the sideboard so near her that she could hear what they were saying.

" Yes, it is sixteen years," one of them replied, in answer to something that she h ad not caught.

" Sixteen   years—that   is   a   long   time.   Sir Ralph was a bachelor then."

" Yes ; he used to give dinner parties, not balls."

" You must find some things changed."

" Not everything, as I feared.   This room, for instance, looks almost exactly as it used, but not quite.   It seems to me that I miss something."

The old gentleman, whose yellow face betokened him a recent arrival from India, gazed inquiringly around.

" I don't see anything altered," said his companion.

" I have it—to be sure.   It is the fowling-pieces, don't you remember ?"

" Hush !" exclaimed the other, lowering his

voice and catching the speaker by the sleeve. "That's Miss Hartley."

He whispered something that Edith could not hear, and then they hastily moved away, looking much disconcerted.

What could there be in the mention of fowling-pieces, so harmful to Isabel? Edith lost herself vainly in conjectures.

She had not yet succeeded in framing any satisfactory explanation, when Lord Skeffington came towards her.

She had paid little attention to his appearance when Isabel had presented him, but now she saw him to be a slender, washed-out looking young man, with high Roman features, and a very attenuated mouth.

"The evening is half over, and my turn is yet to come," he began, in the languid tone familiar to the ears of party goers. "Cruel in Miss Hartley, it was, 'pon my word, to turn me off in this way."

And Lord Skeffington looked as if he consi-

dered Edith must be quite overcome by his pro-
fessions of disappointment.

Edith roused herself.

"You think your dance ought to have been
over a long time ago," she replied, with a furtive
smile.

"Ah now, 'pon my word, Miss Arden, you're
too severe, positively you're too hard upon me.
It's quite too much for a shy man like me. I
can't recover myself at all after a speech like
that, I'm dashed for the whole evening. I'm
quite an object of compassion now, I am indeed,
I assure you. I had a hundred things to say,
and you've driven them all out of my head; quite
crushed, I am."

"You are staying in the house, I believe,"
said Edith, who did not perceive any particular
amusement to be derived from Lord Skeffington's
complaints.

"Yes, Lady Tremyss was so good as to say she
could put us up, so Seyton and I came down.
Queer rambling old place it is, too.   Miss

Hartley tells me it's haunted, and she proposed to put me into a chamber that hasn't been used for centuries;—all full of horrid stories the the place is, it seems;—that chamber belonged to an amiable lady who gave her husband too heavy a sleeping draught one fine night."

"Yes, I know the story," replied Edith; "and are you really going to sleep there."

"I? you can't think it. Of course I'm not. I told Miss Hartley I'd rather sleep on the sofa in the dining-room. Anything better than to sleep in a room that has seen murder. There goes Lady Tremyss," he added, interrupting himself, "Beautiful woman she is, quite beyond her daughter."

While he spoke, Lady Tremyss disappeared in the dancing-room.

"How very pretty," said Edith, as a delicate figure in white crape, caught up with frosted ivy leaves, flitted by. "Who is she?"

"That girl? Oh, it's Miss Eskdale. Her engagement with Tiverton is just off, you know."

"No, I have heard nothing of it," said Edith. "What broke it off?"

"It was the fault of science," replied Lord Skeffington, gravely. "You see Tiverton's uncle wrote a book on gases, or something of the sort, and got elected one of the Royal Society, and was always making experiments, and blowing himself up, and that sort of thing, you know; and Tiverton, who lived with him, got a taste for it, and when his uncle died nothing would do but that he must take his place in the Society; and so he goes to work harder than ever, and he has nearly blown the house up twice—all the fire engines out, and the whole neighbourhood in an uproar, and women and children screaming outside, and Tiverton inside, one mass of cuts and bruises; and the girl didn't like it, you know."

"Very naturally."

"Well, yes, it was rather natural, especially as three doctors out of five said he'd be blind for life, the second time. Her father told him he didn't want his daughter to marry a man who might be found scattered over the neighbouring house-tops any day, and that he must make up his mind to give up chemistry, or the young lady."

" And it seems he chose the latter alternative," said Edith, glancing at the white dress and ivy leaves.

" Well, yes—I can't say I admire his taste, but that's what he did. He said that he could find other wives, but that there was but one theory of combustion, and that he couldn't abandon."

" Poor girl," said Edith, compassionately.

" Not at all ; don't pity her, I beg. She took it as coolly as possible ; but Tiverton did really care for her, for all he was so dead set on chemicals ; and the very next day he made a false calculation, or something of the sort, and there was the devil to pay, again, in his laboratory, and one of his fingers is gone now."

" You think that the most serious feature of the case. Perhaps you are right."

" Oh, yes, of course. She had an escape, I assure you. There's no safety for any woman in marrying any of these one-idead men. An aunt of mine, Lady Jane Grant, tried it once." Lord Skeffington here shook his head, with an air of profound commiseration.

" Was her husband also devoted to chemistry?"

" No; but it was quite as bad; indeed, I think it was worse. He had an idea that persons were different only because of circumstance, and that every one might be educated into a moral and reasoning being. He insisted upon trying the experiment in his own household; and as his theory was that nothing but kindness was to be employed, you can imagine the consequences. They had ticket-of-leave footmen and grooms, and returned convicts for butler and coachman. Lady Jane had frights enough in three months

to turn her into an idiot.   She found the footmen
everywhere—in her bathing tub, behind the fire-
board, and at length on top of the bed canopy."

" How dreadful!" exclaimed Edith.   " What
did her husband say?"

" Sir Murdoch only declared that they were
under the influence of a periodical disturbance of
the sense of right and wrong ; and declared that
the moon was to blame for it, and not the victims
of moral hallucination, as he persisted in calling
them.   However one morning all the servants and
the new butler, a recent arrival from Van
Dieman's Land, and all the plate, were gone,
whereupon Lady Jane formally announced to Sir
Murdoch that she would file a bill of separation
if he ever brought any more moral experiments
into the house, and so he had to give in."

" It is strange the police did not interfere."

" Oh, Sir Murdoch kept it all very close, I
assure you.   He would have felt it quite an
indignity if any one had presumed to find out
anything about his domestic dramas.   He always

did justice himself by means of hot mustard footbaths, and medicine and blood-letting, in order to draw the humours from their brains, as he called it. And they had to submit to it all, because they were afraid of getting into the hands of the police Oh, it was quite an Inferno, it was, 'pon my word. But that is the waltz, I think," he added, as the measure of the music changed. " Seyton will be quite cut up at having missed his quadrille. He has been looking for you everywhere. May I?" And he offered Edith his arm.

She danced that dance, and the next, and many succeeding dances, with many succeeding partners; tall, short, heavy, or amusing, as the case might be.

At length the ball broke up. The carriages rolled away in rapid succession; the musicians left their flower-hidden stand, and retired to their private supper; the wax lights had reached their sockets; the flowers were beginning to droop.

" It is all over," said Isabel, looking around

the deserted dancing-room, where she was standing alone with Walter and Edith; "but it has been very pleasant. Give me a bud from your bouquet, to remember it by."

"Hold it for a moment while I take off my glove," said Edith. Drawing off her glove, she extricated a bud with its leaves from the bouquet.

"Edith," said Mrs. Arden's voice from the adjoining room. "We will go now, my dear, if you're quite willing. It's so late. I'm frightened to think of it."

The two girls left the dancing-room. Walter walked up and down, waiting till his aunt and Edith were ready. The sound of the gay voices of the party staying in the house came from one of the rooms beyond. Suddenly he saw a glove where Edith had been standing. He remembered that she had taken it off to detach the rose. He seized it, and placed it in his bosom.

He did not hear Lady Tremyss' noiseless step in the room behind him. He did not see the reflection of her still face and searching eyes in the mirror, watching him. Before he had turned his head she had glided away. He found her in the drawing-room when he went to take his leave.

" Wait till I bring you your glove," said Isabel.

She ran into the dancing-room.

" Very odd. It's not there," she said, returning.

" I must have dropped it somewhere else," replied Edith. " It's no matter."

Lady Tremyss cast a furtive look on Walter. He remained silent.

Edith and young Arden left the Park, unconscious that their future lay in the grasp of Lady Tremyss.

When Edith and Mrs. Arden reached the Hall, they found Walter waiting for them in the drawing-room. He approached Edith, as Mrs. Arden rang the bell.

" Will you forgive me ?"

She bowed her head, and closed her eyes, to hide the quick tears that rose at his voice.

"I will speak to him—I will tell him that I have nothing to forgive," she thought desperately to herself. She looked up—Walter was gone.

"I am quite surprised; really I don't know at all what to think of it," said Mrs. Arden to Edith, when she appeared at the luncheon table the next day—she had been forbidden over night to get up to breakfast—"Walter has gone to London on business, and doesn't know when he shall be back again. But, gracious, my dear child, how pale you look! how dreadfully your colour has gone! That ball was too much for you, quite too much, I'm afraid," and Mrs. Arden mentally rescinded her resolution as to the dance, leaving some dinner parties for the moment in abeyance.

"Not at all. I feel perfectly well," said Edith. "Yes, it is rather strange he should be called away so suddenly; but business accounts for everything."

She took her place, and drank a glass of water.

"What a charming party it was, wasn't it? and how pretty Isabel looked," Edith resumed, and she proceeded to discourse upon the ball, giving evidence of such good spirits, united to such a keen perception of the ludicrous, as to greatly delight her aunt.

"Well, I have not enjoyed myself so much for a long time; I haven't really," she said, as she laid aside her napkin and rose from the table. "I'd much rather hear you tell about the ball than go to one myself. You are a better mimic than Isabel."

Edith, going upstairs to her own room, shut herself in, until summoned to receive Miss Hartley.

"Gracious, how white you are looking!" exclaimed her visitor, as Edith entered the sitting-room. "I hoped you weren't tired at all. I met Mrs. Arden in the hall, and she said she had never seen you in such good spirits. Ah! now you look more like yourself," she added, as the colour rose to Edith's face.

" Do 'you know, such an unlucky thing happened to-day. One of the grooms was carrying
the letter-bag, and his horse cast a shoe and fell
lame, and the mail had gone, and he had to bring
the bag back again, and your father won't get
mamma s note of thanks till to-morrow. He
will think us savages."

" Not quite," replied Edith. " He will know
there was some mistake."

" That's the only disagreeable thing that has
happened," continued Isabel. " Wasn't it nice,
and didn't everyone look pleased?"

" It wasn't quite so bad, after all, being seventeen, was it?" said Edith, forcing a smile.

" I don't know that," answered Isabel, with
sudden gravity. "I have only been seventeen
one day. But if all the days were to be like
yesterday, I should want never to be anything
but seventeen. I do so love waltzing. Did you
ever know anything so delightful as the way
Walter waltzes?"

"He waltzes well," replied Edith, stooping to look for her india-rubber.

"Oh, it's more than well; he waltzes to perfection. It is no effort to waltz with him. He carries you round. Didn't you find it so?"

"Yes."

"I mean to have another dance next week, just a little one, only the nearest neighbours, to learn the *pas Ghika*."

"You must not count on Walter. He has gone to London, and doesn't know when he will come back," said Edith, steadying her voice.

Isabel sat silent a moment.

"We must find some other good dancer," she said. Then drawing out her watch, "How late it is. I must go. I only came for a moment. Good-bye," and without giving her customary kiss to Edith, she left the room and galloped homeward.

She sprang unaided from the saddle when she reached the Park, and throwing the reins to the groom, ran hastily upstairs to her chamber. She was stifling. What a horrible sensation in her throat. She tore open the breast of her riding-habit, cast a quick, affrighted glance around, and burst into tears. Suddenly she checked them.

"What am I crying for? I don't know. I am a fool!" she exclaimed, impetuously.

She changed her dress, unassisted, smoothed her hair, and descended to the drawing-room, where Lady Tremyss sat, bending over her embroidery frame.

Isabel moved restlessly about the room, taking up and laying down one object after another. At last, selecting a book at random, she sat down and began to turn over its leaves. Their rustling ceased after a while. She was reading. Presently, through the stillness, came the drop of a heavy tear, another and another. Isabel laid down the book and left the room.

As the door closed Lady Tremyss came gliding from the window, took up the book, and sought

through it, till she found the tear-stained page:
"The Bridge of Sighs." What painful associa-
tions could Isabel possibly have with the "Bridge
of Sighs?"

She read it.

" Not only in that old Venetian city,
  Betwixt the prison and the palace wall,
  Oh, Bridge of Sighs, across the sullen water
    Doth thy dark shadow fall.

Athwart the deep-scaled current of our being,
Close hid from curious glance of strangers' eyes,
Close hid from pitying ken of those who love us,
  Rises our Bridge of Sighs.

Across its arch, in endless, sad procession,
Have gone, still pass, and shall for ever tread,
Our weeping hopes, with slow reluctant motion,
  To join the silent dead.

The gladsome visions of our childish morning,
The soft, sweet promise of our youthful day,
The noble aspirations of our noontide,
  All, sighing, pass that way.

We kneel, we stretch our longing arms towards them,
With wild entreaty and imploring moan;
In vain.—The echo of their footsteps ceases,
  And we are left alone.

Alone beside life's dark, fast flowing river,
Whilst through the bitter tears that dim our eyes,
We see the pageant of our hearts' desires,
  End on the Bridge of Sighs."

As she laid down the book, the sound of music came from a distance—a wild mournful melody. It ceased abruptly.

Lady Tremyss pressed her hands to her forehead, and groaned.

When mother and daughter met at dinner, Lady Tremyss furtively studied Isabel's face. There was a startled glance in the girl's eyes, an unquiet quivering about her lips. She looked like a child aroused from slumber, who fears some painful dream may yet be true. The dinner passed almost in silence. Isabel appeared absorbed in her own thoughts. Lady Tremyss spoke at length.

" You saw Edith ?"

Isabel roused herself.

" Yes."

" Was she tired ?"

" She looked so, but Mrs. Arden told me she had never seen her so gay as she was this morning."

" Did you see Walter ?"

"No."

Lady Tremyss asked no more questions.

"What are you doing, Mamma?" asked Isabel that evening, as she saw her mother busy with pencil and paper.

"Writing a list for the dance you said you wanted to give, to practise the new step. Are these all?" She read the names aloud. "There are just enough gentlemen for the ladies."

"Then you will have to ask another man. Walter has gone to London."

Lady Tremyss turned a sidelong look upon her daughter.

"Why did you not tell me so when I asked if you had seen him?"

A vivid flush spread over Isabel's face. "I don't know," she answered hesitatingly, moving away. She soon returned and leaned over her mother's chair.

"I am tired with being up so late last night, Mamma. I think I will go to bed." Her voice trembled. "Kiss me, Mamma, take me in your arms and kiss me as, you used to do when I was a little child."

And Isabel, the child just waking into womanhood, nestled into her mother's arms, and clung around her neck.

As Lady Tremyss pressed her lips to her daughter's cheek, she raised her eyes with the fierce look of a tigress watching over her young, and gazed steadily before her. She was mentally crouching for her spring. —Isabel loved Walter. Walter loved Edith. Walter and Edith must be separated.—

The means were easy of management. Mr. Arden, in the overflow of his gratitude, had called frequently at the Park when staying at the Hall during Edith's illness. She had detected his dislike of his nephew, she had perceived his ambition and vanity. In the conversations he had had with her, she had divined his intentions with regard to Edith. It needed but a word to her father, and she would be instantly removed from the Hall. And the letter that had missed that morning, that must be sent on the morrow :—it gave her the desired opportunity. The dark, cold eyes glittered as she thought of the chance that had placed Walter's secret in her hands.

No sooner had Isabel left the room than Lady Tremyss sat down to her writing table, and in her sharp, Italian hand, wrote to Mr. Arden.

She explained the cause of the delay of her missive, she expressed her admiration of his taste and her high appreciation of his *gracieuseté*, she regretted he had not been present on the preceding evening, she extolled Edith's beauty and distinction, she mentioned the general admiration she had attracted, then touched upon Walter's evident *tendre* for her, (Lady Tremyss, though speaking English perfectly, wrote it like a highly educated French woman,) hinted what an advantageous match it would be for him, and concluded with a hope that they might soon have the pleasure of again seeing Mr. Arden in Warwickshire.

CHAPTER II.

THE next morning brought a note from Isabel, saying that she could not come over to the Hall for her usual ride, and Mrs. Arden proposed that Edith should accompany her on two visits she was to pay that afternoon.

"It will do you good, my dear, to be in the fresh air, and to get a little colour into your cheeks. I never should have thought that one ball could have made you look so wretchedly, I shouldn't indeed, used to them as you are; for you always sat up at Arden Court, didn't you?"

"Always," replied Edith, absently.

"I don't believe they did you any good. I

should be sure to have the headache the next day if I didn't take a dose of sweet spirits of nitre as soon as I came home. Did you ever try it, my dear? It's such an excellent thing."

" Very likely," responded Edith, without any clear idea of what her aunt was talking about.

"But I don't know whether the sweet spirits of nitre would have been the thing after all," continued Mrs. Arden, turning her eyes anew on Edith's face. "I am afraid, my dear, you are beginning to find the Hall rather dull, I really am." Edith was listening now. "And I am sure I don't know what to do about it," added her aunt in a tone of profound perplexity. "You seemed dull before the ball, very; and when it came, it only set you up for one day; and I think now you are duller than before. It can't be very pleasant for you living here with only Walter and me, I know, accustomed as you are are to so much company; but then you see we haven't got the people, my dear."

" I never was so happy in all my life as I have

been at the Hall," exclaimed Edith, bursting into tears, to the great discomposure of Mrs. Arden, who listened to her irrepressible sobs with sensations of helpless remorse.

As Edith retreated to her room, her aunt looked after her solicitously.

"She wants change, I'm afraid. I read the other day that some persons' lungs continually require fresh oxygen. I'm sure other persons' spirits do. I wonder if she is homesick!" Mrs. Arden's eyes vibrated rapidly as they always did when she was making up her mind. "That is it, I'll be bound. To be sure it is. I might have thought of it before. And she is so good and dutiful, she would never express a wish against her father's. She would stay here as long as he wanted. She was happy enough at first, but now she wants to go home. It is natural, after all. However, I can't say anything about it. John Arden might think I wanted to get rid of her." Mrs. Arden paused, and heaved a deep sigh.

" How I wish she could have taken some of Lady Pettigrew's Panacea !"

" Where are you going this afternoon, Aunt ?" asked Edith, as she was about to dress for the drive, " and what shall I wear ?"

" We are going to Lady Chatterton's and Mrs. Lacy's, my dear ; and you had better put on your prettiest things,—not for Lady Chatterton, she would not know or care, but Mrs. Lacy thinks of nothing so much as dress," except flirting, Mrs. Arden might have added, but, being good-natured, did not. " What is it your father sent you that you have not yet worn ?"

" What carriage dress?   A Russian pelisse of light grey and ermine, with a dress and muff like it, and a blue capote."

" That will do very well, very well indeed."

Edith withdrew to assume the winter costume which was to impress Mrs. Lacy.

As she descended to the hall where her aunt was standing, Mrs. Arden's face beamed with pleasure.

" Well, really, I never saw anything so pretty as that, never in all my life. And little grey boots trimmed with ermine to match," she added, smiling, as Edith's downward motion revealed her coquettish *chaussure*. "And it suits you very well indeed, I am sure."

" Yes, Ma'am, doesn't it?" interposed Nitson, who had followed Edith, apparently through sheer inability to detach her eyes from her young mistress's person. " And that caput (unconsciously tracing the appellation to its root), that caput, Ma'am, is just the most perfect thing that was ever put together."

Here Nitson hastily retreated; her habitual respect for time and place, forgotten for a moment, suddenly returning upon her in full force.

The road led by Ilton Park. As they passed the sphinxes at the gate, Edith remembered for the first time the conversation she had overheard in the supper room, and the incomprehensible perturbation of his companion, when the old India gentleman alluded within Isabel's hearing

to the fowling-pieces that had formerly ornamented the walls.   She asked an explanation
of Mrs. Arden.

"I really don't know, my dear.   It was a
shocking case, very.   I was away at the time
that it took place; but I remember that Captain
Hartley, Lady Tremyss' first husband, shot himself accidentally while staying at the Park, but
whether he was out shooting, or how it happened,
I can't recall just now.   They must have been
referring to that."

"I wish I could find out," said Edith.

"It's very easy to find out, my dear; very easy
indeed.   If you really care about knowing, I will
ask Lady Chatterton ; she always knows about
everything, and likes to tell what she knows.
She will tell you all about it, I'm sure."

As Mrs. Arden predicted, so it turned out.
Lady Chatterton, a little, wizened, lively old
woman, with gold spectacles, and a face whose
construction put one irresistibly in mind of a
chameleon, did know all about the circumstances

of Captain Hartley's accidental death, and went off into a detailed account of the same as soon as Mrs. Arden's question had turned the stop-cock of her flow of conversation.

"Oh, yes, it was a dreadful thing, poor young man, so gay and handsome as he was—and his beautiful young wife—it was really a most shock-ing thing, and a dreadful blow to Sir Ralph. He was a changed man after it. Some people thought that seeing such a dreadful catastrophe happen close to his door, actually inside of it, set him thinking about his spiritual concerns, for he had lived hard in his youth, you know, and was a call to a better life; for he quite changed after it, as I say, and went away from the Park and didn't seem to take an interest in anything except securing the poor young wife's pension, for she hadn't a penny, you know. Captain Hartley's family had quite cast him off, on account of his marriage, I believe it was, and he was nothing but a second son, and had nothing in his own right. And for all the pains Sir Ralph took, he couldn't get the pension for her. He was a long time at it; but, somehow or other, the papers were wrong, and so there she was, quite destitute, poor thing, with her little girl. Miss Hartley was about three years old then. When Sir Ralph found that he couldn't get anything out of government for her, he married her himself. And although I always thought and said that he had married her out of pure compassion, yet he certainly was very fond of her afterwards, and it wasn't wonderful either, for she was and is the handsomest woman I ever saw."

"But about Captain Hartley's death," interposed Mrs. Arden, taking advantage of a momentary gasp of Lady Chatterton's.

"Oh, yes, to be sure—poor young man. How little I thought when I saw him at church on Sunday that before the week was out he would be brought in his coffin into that very church for burial. And the church was full. Sir Ralph was chief mourner. His face was as white as a pocket handkerchief, and his eyes were sunk all into his head. He looked as if he hadn't closed his eyes since. And when the earth was cast into the grave on the coffin, for it wasn't put into the Tremyss tomb, as every one expected it would be, he shook all over as if he had the palsy. No one had thought he was a man of much feeling before, but after that, people began to think that they had done him wrong, and he stood much higher. And he hadn't known Captain Hartley so long either. He met him at Gibraltar where Captain Hartley was in garrison, only a few months before, and it was then that he gave him and his wife the invitation to come and stay with him whenever they came to England. And he treated them as if they were the greatest people in the world; there was a dinner party or something every day, ladies' dinner parties for Mrs. Hartley. She used to dress very simply in those days. She used to wear white muslins, with coloured ribbons, and though she was married, yet she looked so very young that they did not seem at all inappropriate. The ladies couldn't tell what to make of her at first, she was so still and silent, but she always had a very fine manner, much the same as it is now, and any one could see that she was clever, though she didn't talk, and they soon liked her. Sir Ralph, as I said, used to treat her as if she were a princess; you know when he chose, and he always did choose in his own house, he could be delightful."

"But how long had they been staying there when the accident happened?" asked Mrs. Arden, abandoning the system of direct questioning, and attempting to bring Lady Chatterton to the point by a change of tactics.

"Oh, they had been there, let me see, it must have been two or three months; it is so long ago that I can't exactly remember. I know that the leaves were on the trees when they came there, and that they were gone the day he was buried. I remember thinking what a sad day it was for a burial, a cold gray sky, and a drizzling rain and bare branches. They said he looked as if he were only asleep when he was lying in his coffin—

people who die of gunshot wounds always look so, I have heard. I suppose they don't have any time to be afraid. And it was a most extraordinary thing, and shows how careful people always ought to be—neither Sir Ralph nor any one else knew that the gun was loaded. The very next week he had all the others taken down; I suppose from fear of some other accident. You see Sir Ralph and Captain Hartley were sitting over their wine after Mrs. Hartley had left the table, and the conversation seemed to have turned on fowling-pieces, for Captain Hartley took one down and began to examine it. There was something peculiar in its construction, so people said, and Sir Ralph prized it very much; and it was that very piece Captain Hartley was examining, and it went off and shot him through the heart."

"How dreadful," exclaimed Edith.

"He fell where he was standing, just in front of the great side-board, and never moved again. They sent for the doctor; though from the first moment they knew there was no hope; but Sir Ralph would have everything done."

" And his wife ?" asked Edith.

" She was the first in the room. She never shrieked nor fainted, but knelt by him and held his head. And when the doctor had examined the wound, and said that death must have been instantaneous—it was an awful wound, people said—then she got up without a word, and went upstairs to her room, where Miss Hartley was asleep, and locked herself in. Sir Ralph left the house that very night and went over to Mrs. Hammerthwaite's, and got her to go and stay there, and the day after the funeral Mrs. Hartley went away with her little girl and stayed with Mrs. Hammerthwaite all through the time Sir Ralph was trying to get her pension. He was working about it for months, and at last, when it couldn't be got, he offered himself to her, and she married him. That was about sixteen months after Captain Hartley's death."

" It seems strange that she could have loved

another man so soon after the death of her husband," said Edith.

"Nobody thought she was in love with him,
my dear Miss Arden ; but you know marriages
are made from a great many causes. Mrs.
Hartley had really no choice. She couldn't have
gone on staying with Mrs. Hammerthwaite for
ever, and she hadn't any money to go any where
else. It was the only way out of her difficulties."

Lady Chatterton was here seized with a violent
fit of coughing, such as her harangues usually
ended in, under cover of which Mrs. Arden and
Edith took their leave.

"What a dreadful story that was," said
Edith, as the carriage took the road to Houston
Lacy. "No one that knows it can wonder at
Lady Tremyss' stillness and reserve. Such a
shock as that must be enough to turn a woman
into stone."

"Yes, my dear, I dare say it might have been,
but I believe she was much the same before her

husband's death. Didn't Lady Chatterton say so?"

"Yes; but I can't help thinking that she was mistaken. She could not have always been as she is now. It would be unnatural that such a thing could take place, without changing every feeling she had. To have the person she loved snatched from her in such a way! I wonder it did not kill her outright."

"Dear me, that would have made it a great deal worse—don't you think so? It was quite bad enough as it was, I'm sure; and what with her daughter and Sir Ralph, both so fond of her, I think she did much better to keep on living, and I've no doubt you'll think so some day yourself, my dear," replied Mrs. Arden, who was capable on occasion of taking a practical view of things.

But Edith, who had not yet reached the age of common sense, made no response, and continued to gaze out of the carriage window, thinking what would become of her if a gun should go off and kill Walter; until unable any longer to endure her imaginings, she was forced to take refuge in conversation with her aunt.

" How is it that I have never seen Mrs. Lacy?" she enquired.   " Houston Lacy is not very far from the Hall, is it?"

" Only about seven miles.   She has been paying some visits ; she's always paying visits."

" What sort of person is she?   It seems to me that I have heard the name before."

" Very likely, she always goes up to London for the season.   She's a pretty woman, though she was prettier once than she is now, and she dresses remarkably well."

This was not exactly what Edith wanted to ascertain, but she knew that her aunt was not strong on analysis of character, and so pursued the subject no further.

" We are not far from Houston Lacy now," continued Mrs. Arden.   " It's a very fine place, very."

The commendation was merited. Houston Lacy was in truth a very fine place. A connoisseur's eye might have been shocked by the irregular architecture of the house, but the general effect was decidedly imposing. The carriage road ended under an enormous porch of glass, which was commanded by the windows of a most luxurious room, too large to be called a boudoir, too small to be called anything else. In this room sat Mrs. Lacy, in the most elegant of morning dresses, consulting the pages of the little memorandum book she held in her hand. On a couch, at a little distance, lounged a *blasé* looking man of about thirty-six, her brother, Ormanby Averil. Brown hair, whiskers, and moustache, regular features, sallow complexion, indolent eyes, tall, rather slender figure, perfectly dressed; and an air of contemptuous indifference; besides these, a large fortune in hand, an earldom, and fifty thousand a year in prospect, only one life in the way, and that one which might disappear at any moment, for the present Earl was very old;—

such were the possessions, present and prospective, of Mr. Averil. But these were not alone sufficient to have given him his autocratic position in society; for his word was the law of fashion, from his judgment there was no appeal. Why he was thus able to tyrannize over the fashionable world, no one knew. Perhaps his fastidiousness, his *nonchalance*, his scarcely-veiled insolence, were the elements of his success. But the fact was indisputable. Society had chosen him its dictator, and obeyed his behests.

" I am sure I don't know what to do," said Mrs. Lacy, laying down her memorandum book. " I invited these people on purpose to please you, and now you say it will be dull."

" Excuse me, I did not say precisely that."

" What did you say then? "

" I said it would be insufferably dull."

" I don't see how that mends the matter," responded Mrs. Lacy, shutting the clasp of her book with a snap.

" I don't see that it does," replied her brother, in a tone of exasperating indifference.

" Do you know, Ormanby, you are getting atrocious. You don't seem to think that a person exists worth looking at."

" Do you think so? "

" I am sure of it. I should think you would die of sheer ennui."

" Perhaps I may. It's not unlikely." He suppressed a yawn.

" Why don't you do something to wake yourself up? Why don't you fall in love? "

" Every one does not find it so easy—" He paused. His mocking smile pointed the sentence.

Mrs. Lacy pushed her chair back from the fire. He had stung her, but she did not dare to express her vexation.

" You have had a good deal of experience, nevertheless," was all she trusted herself to say.

" You surprise me. I was not aware of it."

" Do you mean to say that you have not had more flirtations than I can remember? "

" Possibly, but I thought you were speaking of falling in love."

" People have no business to flirt except they are in love," rejoined Mrs. Lacy, who had a private code of morality of her own.

" I know that is your maxim," said Mr. Averil.

" Don't be so provoking, Ormanby, now don't. I am talking seriously, and you don't seem to know it."

" I desire nothing better than to please you. I will be as serious as you like," answered her brother, looking at her for the first time during the conversation.

" Well, then, seriously, why don't you try to find some object, great or small, in life; something to hang an interest on? It is really melancholy to see you going on from year to year, with just that same indifference and carelessness, as if you didn't care if the world came to an end the next moment."

" You express it admirably. That is precisely the case."

"Then why don't you try to fall in love? It is time you were married."

"I have never seen a woman I could fall in love with, since I was twenty-two."

"And a pretty affair you made of it," retorted Mrs. Lacy, incautiously. "Poor Clara!"

Her voice trembled on the name.

"Take care, Ellen," said her brother.

The sudden expansion of his eye, the quivering of his moustache, showed that the capability of violent emotions lurked under the languid calm of his manner.

Mrs. Lacy was silent a moment, then she answered, in a low tone,—

"I am sorry. I didn't mean to vex you, but I was so fond of her."

It was the remembrance of that affection which now softened Mr. Averil's manner, and unclosed his lips.

"I will speak frankly to you, Ellen, if you wish. I am nauseated with women :—their unveiled eagerness to attract me, not for my own sake,

but for the sake of what they will g et by marrying me; their coquetry, the systematic way in
which they trample down everything like genuine
feeling—those of them that were born capable of
i t—their jealousies, their appetite for admiration,
t heir selfishness, their duplicity, all that I see
low and base in them, has fairly sickened me
with the sex."

" You are unjust, Ormanby; you go into
extremes.   I dare say they want to marry you,
but I don't see that you have any right to say
it is only because they want the position they
would get."

" I have the right given by long experience
of women. I know them."

" Then why not try political life?   You know
you could command a seat at any time you
chose."

" To succeed there, a man must have faith.
He must believe in what he says. I should not."

" There is diplomacy."

" The greatest bore of all."

As if to put an end to the conversation, he called Mrs. Lacy's pet spaniel, which lay curled up on a cushion by the fire.　The creature unwillingly raised its head, opened and shut its eyes, then in obedience to Averil's steady gaze, came and sat before him, looking up with an enquiring expression.

"Go back," he said.

The perplexed spaniel returned to the cushion, and lay down with its eyes fixed upon its summoner and repulser.

"Why did you do that?" said Mrs. Lacy.

"For practice."

"Ormanby, I don't understand you.　Do you know I believe, *au fond*, you are thoroughly unscrupulous."

"Really."

"Yes, I do.　I believe if you ever wanted a thing you would allow nothing to stand in your way."

"Then why advise me to want anything?"

"I dare say I made a mistake, I make mistakes

all the time," confessed his sister, disturbed into candour.

" Mrs. Arden, Miss Arden," proclaimed the footman, throwing open the door. Mrs. Lacy rose to receive her visitors.

Averil's name was not new to Edith. She knew that he was very much looked up to, that her father always invited him, and that he never came. She turned her eyes frigidly upon him, as Mrs. Lacy named him to her, forced so to do by the smallness of the room, which left him no means of escape—, and withdrew her momentary gaze with an expression of haughtiness. She did not like him, he looked cold and selfish ; Mrs. Lacy was better. And she directed her look to her hostess, apparently unconscious that there was any Mr. Averil in the room.

Left to himself, he employed the leisure thus afforded him, in studying his sister's younger visitor. He deliberately examined her delicate features, noted the colour of her hair, the length of her lashes, the grace of her attitude, the peculiar and becoming style of her toilette, and the general distinction of her appearance. She was a beautiful creature, there was no doubt about that. Who could she be? Mrs. Arden had no daughter. But John Arden, the million-aire, he had heard that he had a daughter, not yet out, who promised to be a great beauty. Could this be she? Strange if it were so. Such a man could hardly hàve a daughter like that, he thought, recalling Mr. John Arden's attempts to entrap him into breakfasts, luncheons, dinners, concerts, and balls. At any rate he would find out.

"You have heard recently from Arden Court?"

"Yes."—With a slight inclination of the head, and a downward droop of the eyelids.

"Mr. Arden was quite well, I hope."

"Quite well."—There came no "thank you," to close the sentence.

"A charming place it is, I am told."

Averil's tact was at fault. The "I am told," pointed too plainly to the fact that he had never been there himself.

"It pleases me, of course," was the only reply he obtained, and the long lashes maintained their inclined position immoveably.

Averil tried all those subjects to which he had hitherto found young ladies lend a willing ear. He obtained but a coldly courteous attention. He could not succeed in interesting her. She actually looked bored, as he perceived with indignant surprise. The spaniel came to his relief. It advanced from its cushion, stood wriggling a moment before Edith, then put its fore paws on her lap. She smiled, and patted its head.

"Oh, don't let him put his paws on that lovely silk," said Mrs. Lacy. "His claws are so sharp."

Edith laid down her muff, and motioned with her hand to the dog. It sprang into her lap, curled itself round, and laid down.

Averil returned to his first occupation of gazing at her. Edith, left free, turned her attention from the dog to Mrs. Lacy.

"She will be an irreparable loss, I assure you.

She is the best natured creature in the world, and really clever maids are so apt to be disagreeable; don't you think so?" addressing the last part of her sentence to Edith.

Edith, remembering Brenton still enthroned at Arden Court, gave a full assent.

" I want to get her a good place; for after all she has a perfect right to leave me if she wishes. And I suppose since she has her sister in London, it is hard for her to be away nine months in the year. Don't you want her, so close to London as you are? Félicie is a perfect treasure."

" My maid is not that at all," replied Edith, " but I must ask papa before I can take another."

" I think your father would be quite willing, my dear; I feel quite sure he would," said Mrs. Arden, who, though not admitted into Edith's confidence, had drawn her own conclusions from the fact of Brenton's return to Arden Court without having been allowed to enter her young lady's sick room."

" I hope he will," replied Edith, firmly.

Averil listened. Then, with all that keen penetration and cold decision, she was docile. Had he not made a mistake in his mortifying treatment of her father? He would accept his first invitation. He wanted to study that girl; he liked to see something so peculiar, so different from other people.

"Very *distinguèe*," said Mrs. Lacy, as the door closed upon her visitors.

"Who, the old lady or the young one?"

"The young one, of course,—but it is time to dress for dinner."

CHAPTER III.

COULD Edith have but known that the business which called Walter to London, resolved itself into the search of paintings of North American flowers, she would have felt a little consoled for his abrupt departure. She had expressed before him a wish that she had some of Mr. Hungerford's to copy; and when the sleepless night that succeeded Lady Tremyss' ball had convinced young Arden of the impossibility of remaining under the same roof with his cousin, at least until he had been able to bring some order and calmness into his thoughts, he had decided on going to London rather than anywhere else, because in London he might be able to do Edith that one small service.

Walter's quest through the print shops proved unsuccessful. Everything was to be had, save what he wanted. In the midst of his difficulties a happy suggestion shone in upon him. Mr. Hungerford might possibly be in London. If any one could give him information, it would be he. His address would probably be at the Travellers' Club; and at the Travellers' Club Walter found it, — "Number Three, Petryon Court, City, second story." And accordingly, on the next day, he went to seek out Mr. Hungerford, in the extraordinary locality in which he had thought fit to establish himself.

The driver drew up before the entrance to a small paved court, at the end of which stood a large and gloomy structure.

It had been a building of more than common importance in its day. The windows of the ground floor were strongly barred in foreign fashion; but the addition was of recent date.

While glancing over the façade, Arden's attention was attracted by a young and handsome face, which suddenly appeared at one of the grated windows on the left. The dress of the owner of the face was peculiar, and yet not displeasing. A vest of crimson silk covered the upper part of her figure, her abundant black hair was bound in a massive braid around her head. Across her forehead hung a row of golden coins, her neck was clasped by a heavy chain of the same metal. She stood looking forth from the darkness beyond, with a haughty stare. As Walter gazed at this unexpected apparition, an old grey head appeared behind the handsome stone monolith, for such she looked, a wrinkled hand clutched her shoulder, and, with a sullen scowl, she disappeared.

Young Arden ascended the broad and uneven steps. Directly before him was a ponderous door, heavily studded and plated with steel. It formed the only opening on that floor; all the other doors had been walled up. As he was about to mount the staircase, a man, in the dress of an abbé, descended. Walter made his way up stairs, guided more by feeling than by sight, and knocked at a door, the brightness of whose handle seemed to point it out as the probable abode of Mr. Hungerford.

After a moment's pause, it was opened by an individual, in whom, after an instant of perplexity, he recognized the person of whom he was in search, and whom he had last seen dressed in correct European costume, doing the honours of his album of sketches and paintings in Mr. Tracey's drawing-room.

Mr. Hungerford's keen eyes now sparkled from beneath a red fez, his spare figure was enveloped in a Persian caftan of quilted silk, and his feet were encased in Russian boots of soft undressed leather. He looked very comfortable, but decidedly grotesque.

" Glad to see you, very glad to see you," said Mr. Hungerford, shaking Walter cordially by the hand. " Didn't know me at first, nobody does It is the most convenient dress in the world, though it spoils one for anything else. But come in. You find me in my den."

He conducted Walter through a small ante-room into the apartment beyond.

Young Arden turned an astonished eye around as he crossed the threshold.

"A curious place," said Mr. Hungerford smiling. "A sort of visual Babel, is it not?"

The room into which he entered was of great size. The prevailing hue around was dark. Time had sobered the colours of the frescoed ceiling into sombre repose, and had deepened the tint of the floor and walls into a general hue of warm, rich brown. Against this sober back-ground stood forth an innumerable multitude of objects of the strangest and most incongruous nature.

"It's a very odd place," responded Walter; "the most so that I ever saw."

Mr. Hungerford looked around complacently on his treasures, then motioning Walter to a seat, he placed himself opposite, and leaned back with an air of perfect content.

"It must have taken you a long time to get

these things together," said Walter, " for they are not at all in the style of what one usually finds in the curiosity shops."

" That is just it, and it is that which gives them their value to me," replied Mr. Hungerford, looking much pleased. " I obtained every one of them myself of the original owners. There is not an article here that hasn't a story."

" You should write a catalogue," remarked Walter, " and give descriptions."

" I had that idea once, and began it, but it bid fair to be like that of the British Museum, the end cut off; so I gave it up after I had written two volumes and a half. The fact is that I made my catalogue volumes of travels, essays on man- ners and customs, etcetera, and it was too much for me."

" So much the worse for the rest of us," said Walter.

" You are not so sure of that; you might have found it dry," replied Mr. Hungerford, with a smile that openly contradicted his words. " But àpropos of travels, you should have come in five minutes earlier to have met the Abbé Hulot."

" Was that he?" exclaimed Walter. " I met him going out. I wish I had known it."

" You have read his work, of course?"

" Yes; my aunt was wild to get hold of it, and when she obtained it she found her French too rusty."

" So you translated, I understand? His conversation is still more interesting. I am sorry you missed him, especially as he is just leaving London. But I'll tell you how I can arrange it He comes back in a few months, and then I will invite you to meet him at dinner," said Mr. Hungerford, stimulated to an unusual departure from his present hermit life by the liking he had conceived for young Arden.

" I should be glad to meet him. That book isn't much in my line of reading, but I enjoyed it immensely."

" And I'm sure you'll like him. He is as simple as a child, and yet the influence he exerts over savages is something wonderful. You know he is an extraordinary linguist ; the only man living, in fact, who has mastered the dialects of the American continent; but that isn't sufficient to account for his power over them. How he does it, I can't imagine. I've none of that power myself."

"Many persons would call it magnetism, only I don't believe in magnetism," remarked Walter.

"Neither does he, nor I either, for that matter. No ; it is one of those incomprehensible things that one must be content to leave uncomprehended. It is a great pleasure to have him come in upon me as he did just now."

"You have abundance of companions," said Walter, glancing at the book-cases.

"Yes, I'm not badly off there ; and my pencil, too, is a great resource."

"You must have given a great deal of time to it. I never saw such beautiful paintings as those you showed us. I have searched London in vain for paintings of the same flowers."

"I dare say. What did you ask for?"

"Painted engravings of North American flowers."

"Where did you go?"

"To every print-seller's in London."

"You should have gone to Hall and Henderson's, and asked for 'Audubon's Birds of North America.' He gives all the finest varieties of trees and flowers as well."

"Thank you; I shall go to them."

"You will find it there, if anywhere, and a magnificent work it is. Are you going to send out for plants to America? You'll scarcely succeed, I fear. They don't flourish in our climate."

"No; I was not thinking of that; they were for my cousin, Miss Arden, to copy."

"Oh, then she liked them so much? I feel quite flattered. A very charming person, that young lady. I think I have never met with equal sweetness and decision combined."

Walter made no reply.

"And she has, I fancy, what is rare—tenacity,"

continued Mr. Hungerford. " Not the common kind, but that valuable sort which comes from a well-founded confidence in her own judgment."

"You have studied her well, I see," said Walter, with effort.

"It is my *métier* to study character. I should have had my brains dashed out a dozen times if I hadn't. Yes, I quite know that young lady, and, little as I know of her, I count her a valuable acquaintance. There is no weakness in her, I should say—no fear of her ever ' changing her mind,' as women call it. J wish there were more like her," said Mr. Hungerford, who was not a general admirer of the sex.

With those last words came an electrical revulsion in Walter's mind. How or why he knew not, but he felt that he had been mistaken. He had judged her by a few cold words, by a few, perhaps imperfectly comprehended actions. He had allowed these to triumph over and cast into the shade all the many evidences of friendliness— no, he would call it by the right word—of affection, that he had received from her before. And how had he acted? He turned on his chair as if from a sudden spasm;—but he must listen. What was it that Mr. Hungerford was saying? something about somebody on the ground floor.

"He has really a magnificent collection. Between the anxiety of taking care of his stones and of a young wife, whom he brought with him from the Levant some two or three years ago, he seems to lead a miserable life enough. I never saw a more starved-looking object, and he is worth thousands."

"Was that the young woman whom I saw at the window below?"

"It must have been He keeps no servant, he is so afraid of being robbed. She lives there alone with him. I pity her, poor thing. He tried locking her up in the back rooms when she first arrived, but she refused to eat, and starved herself into the front ones. I believe the grates are as much to keep her from getting out, as thieves from getting in."

" He does not literally keep her a prisoner there, does he?" asked Walter.

" Pretty much the same thing. She only goes out on Saturdays, when he takes her to the Synagogue."

" I should think her dress would draw a crowd on such occasions."

"She looks like a street beggar then. He makes her put on the shabbiest clothing."

" How she must hate him!" said Walter.

"I think she would be glad to do him any ill turn she could. But to return to his jewels—he has some of the finest sapphires I ever saw, two or three stellated, really unique."

" I think I will step in as I go down, and see whether I can find anything that pleases me," said Walter, recollecting that he had promised his aunt to choose for himself some trinket the next time he went to town, in anticipation of his approaching birthday.

" You will do well," said Mr. Hungerford

"and be sure that he shows you the stellated sapphires."

Walter took his leave. Descending the dusky staircase, he knocked at the steel-plated door.

A sliding shutter was pushed aside, revealing an iron grating, through which peered the same grey head which Walter had seen before. The Jew studied young Arden's appearance for a while; then the shutter was returned to its place, there was a rattling, clinking sound within; the door was opened, and the dealer, bowing low, signed to Walter to enter.

No sooner had he crossed the threshold than the Jew again barred and chained the door, then conducted him into a small chamber, lighted from above. Around the walls were iron safes, in the centre stood a small table.

"Vot does de young shentlemans blease to vant?" asked the old Jew.

"I wish to see some stones."

"Sall it be diamondsh?"

The old man lingered on the last word, as though each separate syllable imparted to his palate some delicious savour.

" No."

" It ish many or von ? "

" One."

" Ay, for a ring. Vell, ve sall zee."

Locking the door of the room, and opening a safe, he produced a tray, containing several small parcels.

" But I cannot see," objected Walter, glancing at the aperture above.

" Vait von leetle minute," said the Jew, in his detestable jargon. " Ve vill have light—goot light, light enough."

He produced a lamp from a corner.

" Day-light is not goot for zeeing vith," he said, lighting the lamp it and placing it on the table. Then seating himself opposite Walter, he began to unfold his papers. The stones flickered and sparkled as he held them up to the lamp; the old man's eye shone as he handled them and expatiated on their separate beauties.

"Look at dese emerald. Ish not anoder like it in all Creat Pritain, zo dark; and dese zapphiresh. Dey ish plocks of peauty—velvet, plue velvet dey ish, and full of shtars. And dese rubish. Dropsh of blood—zo bright, zo clear."

"Show me something in its setting," said Walter. "I suppose you have things of the sort."

"Oh, yees, every sing de young shentlemans vants."

The Jew replaced the papers and tray, and opened a second safe, much larger.

"It ish von ring all de zame?" he said, turning to Walter.

"Yes."

"Den here ish vot sall satishfy any von."

He unlocked the box, and opened one ring case after another. Walter gazed with an indifferent eye on their contents. He had seen such things before. He wanted something quite different from all these. The dealer watched his face observantly. He opened another safe, drew forth a box, with small pincers detached a stone from its setting, and presented it to Walter.

"Look," he said. "Vas ever any sing zo fine ash dat?"

He held up a stone, not large, but of peculiar hue, and vivid brilliancy.

"What is that? It is very fine."

"Ish it not fine? Ish it not zuperb? Ish it not zblendid?" said the old man, raising his voice at each consecutive word. "Dat ish unique. Got has made no more like it."

The gem was of a deep orange tint, but brilliant as a diamond. It fairly blazed in the light.

"You sall know it by de tashte. Ish von creat zegret. Ish as cold as von diamond, shust ash cold ash de finesht diamond. De young shentlemans sall zee for himself."

He produced several diamonds and urged

Walter to press them in turn to his lips. The stones were cold in exact proportion to their brilliancy. The orange-coloured diamond, as the Jew called it, was as frigid to the touch as the most sparkling of them all."

"Dat ish de zingle vay to know. Ish de Ruzzian vay. No mishtake dere. Zo a plind man sall tell ash vell ash I."

"What is its price?" said Walter.

"Put, my young shentlemans, it hash no brice. It ish peyond a brice—so peautiful a shtone."

"How much do you want for it?"

"Vot sall I zay? It ish de only von."

"If you do not want to sell, why show it?" inquired Walter, impatiently.

"Oh, de young shentlemans ish in too creat hurry. It ish dat 1 musht conzider. De shtone ish vorth—ish vorth—all of two hundred poundsh, put I sall zell it to de young shentlemans for von hundred and twenty poundsh, zo dat ven de young shentlemans ish married he sall come to me for de diamondsh of his lady."

—One hundred and twenty pounds—that was a round sum to pay for a fancy. He would not take the stone at that price. His aunt had told him to spend a hundred, and that was a great deal too much.—The old broker tried expostulation and persuasion in vain. Walter turned on his heel. The Jew called him back.

" It ish von pargain ; it ish von creat pargain," he said, heaving a sigh. " Put de young shentlemans vill come to me for de diamondsh. Of dat I am sure, ven I give it for von hundred poundsh."

On the way to the bookseller's, Walter passed Hunt and Roskell's. He stopped there to choose a setting for the stone.

" Pray excuse me, Sir," said the shopman to whom he addressed himself, " but I should like to call one of the partners. This is quite out of the common way ; a very extraordinary stone for its tint."

He summoned one of the heads of the firm, who examined the gem with interest.

" A very fine stone, Sir, very fine, indeed. Might I enquire where you obtained it?"

" Of a dealer in Petryon Court."

" Precisely—of Ishmael David. He has a good collection, perhaps the best in London. This stone is extraordinarily fine. You were fortunate to obtain it."

" What is it? He called it an orange-coloured diamond, but I know nothing about stones. It was handsome, and so I bought it."

" It is not surprising, Sir, that you did not know it. Few persons would. It is a zircon, and the finest I have ever seen, with one exception. Mr. Daubenay, of Daubenay Manor, has a very old one, almost precisely similar. I remember it distinctly. It was brought here to have the setting made firmer."

As he spoke the jeweller carefully examined the stone anew. He seemed to find something unexpected in it.

" Very strange," he said, as if to himself.

" What is it ?"

The jeweller pointed out an almost imperceptible fracture.

"Mr. Daubenay's stone has a mark like that. I was on the point of discharging the workman into whose hands it was put, for I thought him to blame in the matter; but Mr. Daubenay stated that the mark had always been there. Though so long ago I remember it distinctly, for I was much annoyed at the time."

"That is very odd," said young Arden. "Can this be the same?"

"It seems impossible that the family should allow such an heir-loom to pass from its hands. But it would be easy to verify the fact. As I said, Mr. Daubenay is one of our customers. Should you desire it, Sir, I can write to him."

"Pray do so at once," said Walter. "I can't say that I like the coincidence. What is the character of this dealer?"

"He is a Jew—that is against him, Sir; but I never heard of his getting into any trouble."

"No fear of his being a receiver of stolen goods?"

"Not the slightest, I should say. That he sold it for double what he gave for it is probably certain."

The jeweller cast an enquiring glance at Walter.

"I gave him a hundred pounds for it."

"That would be a fair price for a diamond of that size and water, for the stone is not large."

"I wish I had insisted on seeing the setting."

"Oh, then he had the setting?"

"Yes. He took it out of its setting before he showed it to me."

The jeweller pursed his lips together.

"I think, Sir, it might be as well to telegraph at once to Mr. Daubenay."

"Then I beg you will do so. You have my address, I think. I leave London to-day."

"Arden Hall, Warwickshire. Certainly, Sir.

I will write immediately on receiving the answer."

" Disagreeable business," Walter said to himself, as he drove to the bookseller's.

" ' Audubon's Birds of North America?' Yes, Sir, we have it."

And the shopman began to explore the highest shelves. Apparently he found some unexpected difficulty in discovering the whereabouts of the volumes. He called some other shopmen to his aid. They disappeared into inner recesses, whence they returned with blank faces. At length a middle-aged man was appealed to. He spoke a few explanatory words, then came forward to Walter.

" Very sorry to detain you, Sir. We have only a mutilated copy down stairs. The rest have not been unpacked, but I will have one got down directly. Can I not send it to you?"

" Send it to Fenton's. It must be there by two."

" It shall be there in half-an-hour, Sir."

Walter gave his name, and began to turn over some books. A large red-faced man came out from behind a great desk.

" I thought we had one down here," he said, in a low voice, to the middle-aged man.

" So we had; but they sent from Lambwell's, saying that they had received a telegraphic message for painted engravings of American flowers —order unlimited as to price. There were none in the market, so they sent to us for the plates of an Audubon. I cut them out, and sent them."

" Ah, very well. Do you know where they went ?"

" No; but I have the message."

" The middle-aged man explored among some papers.

" There it is."

He handed it to the red-faced man, who read aloud,—

" Lady Tremyss, Ilton Park, Warwickshire."

Though conducted in a low tone, Walter had

overheard the dialogue.—Rather strange; what could Lady Tremyss want of those plates when she had already such a number as Edith had seen and described to him? But those were old and time-stained, Edith had said. Perhaps she wanted a fresh set.—An inexplicable prompting made him accost the bookseller.

" When was it that you sent down those engravings?"

" About the middle of last month, Sir, I think it was; but I can tell exactly, I have the date." He referred to a book. " It was on the sixteenth, Sir."

The sixteenth! His aunt's dinner party had been on the fifteenth; and the perception of something strange came strongly upon Walter.

When he reached Fenton's the books were already there. He unfastened the parcel and began to look through them. As he turned over the leaves he started and remained fixedly gazing upon a brightly coloured page.—Those blue jays, h knew them, Edith had drawn them the morning after her dinner at the Park.   But she had said the engravings were old and time-stained; and yet they had been sent down only the day before.   What did it mean ?—Walter knit his brows, and compressed his lips, as the perception of something strange deepened upon him.

By the action of some of those finer processes of thought which defy explanation, the remembrance of the catch in the story of the little boy who had watched beneath the bridge on the night of Sir Ralph's death, rose upon young Arden's mind. Where was the connection ?   He could not see it. And yet the two stood side by side before him, with vague and uncertain outlines, shifting as wind tormented clouds, yet with something palpable lurking beneath their misty shroud. Something was there.—What was it?

CHAPTER IV.

IT was on the fourth evening after Walter's departure, that he reached again the Hall. As he drew near, he glanced at Edith's window. It was dark. But the drawing-room was lighted. She was there, with his aunt.—He found Mrs. Arden only.

"Why Walter, is it you? You gave me quite a start."

"Yes. I got through, and here I am back again."

He looked around. How cold, and blank, and dismal, the great apartment looked.

"I'm glad you're come back, very. I was getting quite dismal, all alone. Edith went back with her father, yesterday."

Walter walked to the fire-place, and leaned over the mantel-piece.

" Was it not rather sudden ? " he asked, after a moment.

" Yes. I hadn't any idea of it at all. He hadn't sent any letter or anything, and down he comes, quite unexpectedly, and says Edith is looking nicely, and I'm sure she wasn't, and says that he is going to take her back. It has quite upset me. I had got to be so fond of her, you don't know."

Mrs. Arden proceeded, as Walter made no answer,—

" I know it was the best thing for her. She was home-sick, I know she was home-sick."

" Did she say so ? " asked Walter harshly.

" Oh, no, she said she had never been so happy before, as she had been here, never in all her life, she said."

" Then why do you say such a thing ? " he demanded impatiently.

" Why ? Because I'm sure of it, of course,"

answered Mrs. Arden, a little resentfully, "any-one might see it. She has been pining for home all by herself, until her nerves are quite shaken, quite. She cried when I told her that I was afraid she found it dull here with only you and me, though she answered she had never been so happy before, and she cried the night before she went. And it isn't her way to cry, not at all, and her being so upset showed that something had got on her nerves, and it couldn't have been anything but home sickness, you know."

Walter was silent. Self-reproach was sharpening Mrs. Arden's every word. She went on,—

"And I blame myself, I do indeed, for not having seen before what the matter was. I ought to have known, when I saw her so quiet and grave, after having been so gay and cheerful as she was some weeks ago, you remember?"

"Yes," said Walter, and something like a groan came with the word.

"When I saw her change so, not but what she was always gay at table, and pleasant and bright whenever I spoke to her, but, as I say, when she began to look so sad when she was left to herself, I ought to have seen that she needed change, and to have said so. But I did not think of the home-sickness at first, I only thought she was getting a little tired of being so much alone with us; and afterwards I felt unwilling to say any-thing about it, you know, for fear it should seem like advising her going away. Perhaps I made a mistake, and let her spirits get quite run down; for, as I said, she certainly was not at all like herself at the last, I do not mean the very last, for she drove away with her father, smiling, though she had cried so much the evening before, when she came into my room, that she looked as pale as a ghost, she did, indeed."

A wild desire to blow his brains out rushed through Walter's mind, at this second reference to Edith's anguish at leaving the Hall.—What a brute, what an idiot he had been.—Before he slept that night, he had written a long letter to Edith, the outpouring of a young man's heart.

As Mrs. Arden had said, Edith smiled up at her father as she drove away from the Hall. She chatted with him on the journey, telling him all that she fancied would amuse him. When she mentioned the name of Ormanby Averil, her father's face assumed an expression of great interest.

"Ah, a very distinguished man in society, Mr. Averil, very distinguished. So you met him. How did he strike you?"

Mr. Arden would have asked, "how did you strike him?" could he have done so, but that was inadmissible.

"I did not like him."

"That surprises me. Did he talk to you?"

"Yes."

"What did he say?"

"He asked me if I had heard from you lately, whether you were well, and said that he heard Arden Court was a fine place.'

There was a certain cool, cutting intonation in Edith's voice, as she uttered the words, that made her father feel somewhat uncomfortable. But his pleasure at this indirect advance from a man he had so long courted in vain, triumphed over the momentary annoyance. "Ah, really," he said, in a tone expressive of high gratification, with which, despite himself, mingled the unmistakable alto of surprise.

It was surprising. What could be the reason of so sudden a change? Ormanby Averil had been as haughty and distant as ever when he had last met him. He glanced around, as if seeking from the sides and top of the railway coupé the explanation of so unexpected a phenomenon as politeness from his powerful social enemy; his eyes chanced to fall upon his daughter's face. He started. Was it that? It must be. He looked at her as if he had never seen her before. How beautiful she had grown! What a sensation she would produce! And Mr. John Arden's eye noted the separate charms of his daughter's physique, with a satisfaction not totally alien to that with which a slave dealer would scan the perfections of some new arrival from Georgia, the chief difference being that the slave dealer would count the price in gold, while Mr. John Arden counted it in the increased estimation which would accrue to himself.—It was strange that she should have begun her career before he had thought she was ready for it, and begun it too, by making an impression on such a man. Pity that every one was in the country, and that there would be no chance of bringing Edith and Mr. Averil together for so long a time.—

He was still pondering when Edith spoke.

" Papa, if you please, I should like another maid."

"Certainly, if you wish it," replied her father, " but really I don't see how you can find occupation for two at a time."

" I don't mean that—I would like to send away Brenton."

" That is not to be thought of," said Mr. Arden, with a certain harshness in his tone new to

Edith's ear, though not to her imagination. She had always known that vein to exist in her father's character, though she had been so uniformly docile that she had never touched on it before. "Brenton is invaluable—not to be parted with on any account. Pray what put this in your head?"

"Mrs. Lacy asked me if I did not want her French maid."

"Mrs. Lacy; ah, that is different." Mr. Arden's voice softened at the name.—Mrs. Lacy was noted for her tasteful toilette. Then, too, she was Ormanby Averil's sister. Perhaps, after all, this French maid might be better for Edith than Brenton.—

"Why does she leave her?"

"To be near her sister, who is in London."

"What did Mrs. Lacy say of her?"

"That she was a perfect treasure."

All Brenton's past services counted as nothing in the eyes of Mr. Arden. He valued every one in proportion to what he could get out of them.

Brenton he considered an estimable servant; but if some one else could fill her place better, Brenton must go. So, after brief cogitation, he signified his assent, and gave Edith permission to write to Mrs. Lacy, to engage the services of the French woman.

Edith had left the Hall after luncheon. It was dark when she reached Arden Court. As she drove up the sweep of the avenue, she experienced a strange novelty of sensation. It appeared to her as if she had never seen the house before, as if it were not her home. Her heart sank as though she were entering a prison when she ascended the marble steps which led to the circular, statue-lined hall. She blindly felt the magnificence that surrounded her to be hostile to her happiness.

Her father led her through the drawing-rooms, all white, and gold, and crimson, to a smaller room beyond, which had formerly been all white, and gold, and crimson also.

"This is yours. Do you like it?" he asked. The room was newly furnished with blue and silver. It looked the perfection of comfort and luxury, and Edith poured out her gratitude.

"Yes. Gillow has done it very well. I gave him carte blanche, and told him to make it as handsome as he could."

Edith felt a pang of disappointment.— She had thought—but how foolish and ungrateful she was, —and again she commented on the beauty of everything around.

"Yes, when we get some music on the piano-forte and a drawing on the easel it will do very well. I am quite in a hurry to examine your portfolio," he added. "I see from your letters that you have been busy lately."

It was a favourite desire of John Arden's that Edith should be distinguished for her accomplish-ments as well as for her other advantages, and though she had shown little aptitude for music— hers not being that impulsive Southern tempera-ment which craves an easy vent for its every emotion, but belonging rather to the deeper and more passionate Northern type, which can die for what it loves, but feels no need to say so,— yet her talent for drawing was such as to promise full gratification to his ambition in that direction.

Mr. Arden possessed some knowledge of art, quite inadequate, however, to the sums he had expended in obtaining it ; it was accordingly with an important and magisterial aspect that, when the pompous ceremonial of their *téte-à-tête* dinner was over, he opened his daughter's portfolio and commenced his examination of its contents.

"That is not bad—not bad at all," he said, holding up to the light a sketch of the Roman bridge near the Hall. "It is supposed that our family takes its name from that bridge. We formerly owned it. The derivation is very plain. The mixture of Saxon and Latin in which it originated is interesting, at least in Sir William Digwell's opinion. Den arcus, Denarc, Arcden, Arden."

"But isn't arcus, arch?" inquired Edith.

"My dear, I give you Sir William's opinion. Arch or bridge, it is all the same thing." Edith was silent. Mr. Arden turned over the sheets.

"So you do figures, too. Those are well touched in," he resumed, espying a sketch of the little church with two figures in the foreground, the one a girl sitting on a tombstone, the other a young man standing before her. Edith did not think it worth while to inform him that those figures represented Walter and herself.

"Ah, Mrs. Arden—good, very good indeed," he remarked as he inspected a sketch of that lady.

He lifted another sheet.

"What a shocking thing, my dear. What could have induced you to make this?" And he held up a hastily but powerfully executed crayon head, the head of a negro, seamed with a ghastly scar.

"I did it because I wanted to get used to it," replied Edith.

" What is it ; some character in a book ?"

" No. It is Goliath, the butler at Ilton Park."

" Ah ! it seems to me that I remember. Was there not something about him at the time of Sir Ralph's death ?"

" Yes ; he went into the river to save him."

" Yes; I remember now. I heard it spoken of at a dinner at Lord Plowden's ; a friend of Sir Ralph's was there. He had thrown something at the man and laid his face open. That must have been the way he got that scar," and Mr. Arden glanced again at the drawing. " The trouble was about the key of the wine cellar. It was one of Sir Ralph's freaks that Mr. Manning told of. He had dug a wine vault down to an absurd depth in order to have the wine at the same temperature, summer and winter, and it was that key which was lost. A great many stories were told that evening about Sir Ralph."

" What were they ?" asked Edith.

" Stories about his younger life. They would not interest you, my dear."

Edith perceived she was not to press the question. She wished, nevertheless, that she could know more about Sir Ralph. The evil power depicted in his face had impressed itself strongly on her sensitive imagination. She figured him something Titanic, monstrous. She was almost glad he was not alive.

Mr. Arden continued to turn over the drawings.

"Why, Edith, did you do this?" he exclaimed as he came to a water-coloured sketch of a horse's head. "It is admirable, admirable. I shall show that to Landseer." And, despite Edith's deprecatory entreaties, he separated it from the rest. "Where did you find your model? I never saw so much character in an animal's head." He turned it, and saw a name written on the back of the sheet, "Moira."

"One of Lady Tremyss' horses. Isabel lent her to me."

"But who wrote this name? It is not your writing."

"It is Walter's," replied Edith.

There was an indescribable something in the tone that caught her father's ear. He looked at her. She stooped over the drawings.

Mr Arden, gifted though he was with " business tact," as it is called, was not an acute man with regard to women. Had not his suspicions with regard to Walter been already aroused, it is not probable that he would have paid any further attention to so slight an indication as that conveyed in his daughter's voice. But Lady Tremyss' letter had quickened his perceptions, and enforced upon him the conviction that he had done a most unwise thing in sending his daughter to Arden Hall. In fact, with that blindness which seems unaccountably to affect some parents, especially good-looking men not much past their meridian, he had always continued to look upon Edith as a mere child. Her singular youthfulness of appearance had maintained and confirmed him in this error ; and it was with astonishment almost equal to his indignation that he had gathered from the missive in question, that Edith was considered of an age to receive the serious attentions of young Arden. When he met her, and saw in how surprisingly short a time she had expanded into womanhood, his self-condemning reflections grew still more poignant. Mr. Arden was mentally characterizing himself as a fool, while he was outwardly greeting his daughter with fatherly affection ; and he hurried her from the Hall with impatient precipitation, as if hoping to make up by present haste for past imprudence.

He now determined to go to the bottom of the matter, as he mentally termed it.

"You saw a great deal of young Arden, I suppose."

" At first."

" Not of late ?"

" No."

" What did you think of him ?"

" I don't know precisely what you mean," replied Edith quietly, her heart beating the while almost to suffocation.

" Did you like him ?"

" Yes."

The word was low but firm. Mr. Arden, having arrived at this stage of his enquiries, began to feel perplexed. He did not quite know how to pursue his investigation. He found himself fearing that Edith cared more for her cousin than he had apprehended ; and his wrath against Walter rose like a spring tide.

" Curse him, has he dared to make love to her !" he silently muttered.

Before he put away the confiscated drawing of Moira's head, he attentively examined the handwriting it bore.

The second day's post brought a letter directed to Edith. As usual, the letter bag had been brought into the library where Mr. Arden took his solitary breakfast before starting for the City. He scanned the superscription and post-mark. " Wodeton." And the hand—

He drew out the water-coloured drawing and compared the characters, frowned, took up the letter as if about to break the seal, laid it down again on the table, walked up and down the room, then, again taking up the letter, dropped it into the fire.

As the flame caught the enclosure it crackled and unfolded. The last lines became visible. John Arden read,—

" But if indeed it be so, do not write.   I could not bear it.   Your silence will be enough.

"WALTER ARDEN."

Mr. Arden started when the butler came into the room a few moments later.   He turned a hasty glance upon the fire, as if fearing that the impalpable ashes might form themselves into an accusing phantom of the letter.   He did not look at the man as he gave the orders he had come, according to custom, to receive ; and he omitted going up to his daughter's room that morning before leaving, saying to himself that he feared to disturb her, that perhaps she was asleep.

The return mail brought to the Hall no letter from Edith; the second came in,—still silence. Walter's hopes expired in all the anguish of a violent death.

"It's all over," he said to himself, after he had been sitting a long time without moving, on that second and last day. The words seemed spoken by another person; they had an unreal sound. He raised his head and looked around, as if to assure himself where he was, then took his hat and left the house.

The winter day was drawing to its close. The great black branches of the old chestnut trees stood clearly defined against the pale reflections of the western sky. He turned, half unconsciously, into the path that he had followed on the evening that Edith had arrived. The quiet lane blossomed no longer, no green leaf met his eye. He came out on the open hill-top; he bared his head, and looked around. The desolation of winter rested on the fields;—drear stretches of frozen ground, brown thickets, and skeleton woods. The flush and glory of summer had passed; the earth lay dead before him. There was a hard and rigid look on the young man's face as he gazed. The sun sank, the red glow of its setting paled into dusk, the stars came out; but the hard and rigid look still remained on Walter's face when he turned to retrace his steps.

As he left the lane and passed along the road, two mounted figures met him—Lady Tremyss and Isabel, followed by a groom. They stopped. Lady Tremyss held out her hand. It was not her wont so to do.

"We meet you *à propos;* I want to engage you for next Monday evening. Will you come?"

Walter's first impulse was to refuse; then he remembered that Isabel would probably have heard from Edith. He accepted. Isabel had not spoken; she only bade him good-bye as

she loosened her horse's rein. She was riding
Moira.

"Oh, Walter, a telegraphic message has come
for you. A man brought it over from Wodeton.
What can it be about? I can't possibly imagine,"
said Mrs. Arden, eagerly, as Walter came in.

"From London," he answered, opening
the envelope. It was the first time since his
return that he had thought of the jeweller's
promise to find out from Mr. Daubenay whether
the family jewel was still in his possession.

"Mr. Daubenay has arrived in London—will
be in Wodeton to-morrow."

On the morrow Mr. Daubenay arrived. He
was a tall, spare man, with delicate features, and
courteous address. The deep lines on his forehead showed the frequent presence of anxious
thoughts, the sad compression of his lips indicated
that whatever his grief might be, it sought no
relief in expression.

"We are scarcely strangers, though we have

not met before," he said with a grave smile, in answer to Walter's greeting. "My boy has often spoken of you."

"The best fellow in the world," responded Walter, with a warmth which brought a momentary look of pleasure over the father's face.

"You are aware on what business I come," he said, after a pause.

"With reference to the stone, I presume."

Mr. Daubenay bowed. The lines on his forehead deepened. When he next spoke, it was in a constrained and somewhat harsh voice.

"You may be aware of a very painful circumstance affecting my family, which occurred in Canada many years ago."

Walter made a gesture of assent. Unmistakable sympathy was stamped on his face. Mr. Daubenay's tone softened.

"That ring my brother always wore on his watch-chain. He took it with him to Canada. Since then, with him, every trace of it has been lost. You see of what moment it is to me—to all who love him "—his voice grew husky, " to trace back this clue."

" Certainly," exclaimed Walter, " most certainly. If I could be of any use"—he looked inquiringly at Mr. Daubenay. " If there be anything that I could do—"

" You can be of very material use, if you are willing to come with me to London and confront this Jew."

" We will have luncheon at once," said Walter, ringing the bell. " If we take the next train we shall be in London this evening. Of course you wish to lose no time."

" Certainly not. I was away from home, so that the message was two days in reaching me. I have travelled all night. To-morrow I can procure a search-warrant, and shall probably be able to find where the Jew obtained the stone. It will be a difficult affair to manage," he continued, with a sharp contraction of his brow. " You are aware of the danger."

" If this were spoken of, certainly," answered Walter.

Mr. Daubenay sat silent, gazing into the fire.

"Of course, so long ago, they wouldn't maintain—" Walter stopped. He could not risk the words, "the sentence."

"No similar instance of clemency has ever yet occurred," returned Mr. Daubenay. "It would be rash to expect it." And he fell to musing again.

"Who is it that he looks like?" thought Walter. "Where have I seen those straight delicate brows?" He racked his memory in vain.

The next morning Mr. Daubenay and young Arden, accompanied by a detective, stood outside the steel-plated door of the house in Penryon Court.

The sliding shutter had no sooner been pushed aside in answer to Walter's knock, than it was hastily returned to its place, and no further answer vouchsafed to the repeated summons of the party without.

"Curse the old fox," said the detective, a low-bred but acute-looking man, "he's gone to 'ide it."

"Then that settles it," said Mr. Daubenay. "It must have been stolen."

"No ev'dence, Sir. He may 'ave come by it 'onestly, and 'ide it hall the same, for fear of gettin' hinto a scrape. He got hinto 'ot vater in Paris vunce, and that makes 'im shy."

And he thundered again at the door. This time the appeal was to some purpose. The bars and chains were unfastened and the old Jew appeared,—his eyes looking sharper, and his stature smaller, than when Walter had seen him last.

"Now, Mr. David, you vill be so good as to let us see the setting o' this 'ere stone that this gen'l'man bought o' you four days ago, and that vill save you and us a good deal o' trouble." And so saying, the officer displayed his search warrant. "You see vot ve've got to back us Now be quick."

"Put, my tear shentlemans, I 'ave not got de shetting. I never did 'ave de shetting. Zo as I showed de shtone, zo vas it zold to me by

Abraham Shebbard, vot ish now in Riga. He
zold it to me vour montsh ago. Zo true as Got
himzelf, zo true ish vat I zay."

" There's no use in talking to the hold rascal,"
said the officer, with a look of disgust. " He'd
svear hisself black afore he'd give it up. So,
Mr. David, be so kind as to shove yerself out o'
the vay."

He pushed by the Jew.

" Are you not going to demand his keys?"
enquired **Mr. Daubenay.**

The detective cast back a compassionate
glance.

" Lord love you, Sir, the keys vouldn't be of
no use. He knows better nor that."

So saying the officer began to rummage in every
place most unlikely to be chosen as the hiding-
place of the ring.

" It's lucky there isn't no fire," he remarked
to Walter, as they made the round of the apartments, which seemed quite uninhabited. He cast
a stealthy glance at the Jew as he said it. An

exulting, quickly repressed gleam caught his practised eye. " Let's go back to the front," he said quietly to his companions. They returned to the door of the room where Walter had seen the Jewess. It was a large, desolate looking chamber, into which they had as yet merely glanced. As their steps echoed on the floor, they heard a sound like that of the grinding of a coffee mill. The detective glanced around. The Jew was shrinking out of sight.

" 'Ere, Mr. David, don't be so himpolite as to leave your comp'uy to thesselves," said the officer. " Just come hin agin, hif you please."

As the Jew reluctantly returned, the officer locked the door, and put the key in his pocket.

" Now, Sir, hif you vill please to lend a 'and, I think ve shall come to summat a leetle more hinteresting."

Aided by Walter, he pulled away a large wardrobe, which, being empty, proved to be much less heavy than it looked ; and displayed a narrow door.

" But his wife, where is his wife?" said Walter, remembering the Jewess for the first time.

The Jew muttered a curse between his teeth.

" It's a pity to hinjure a gen'l'man's premises ven it can be 'elped," said the detective, smiling triumphantly. " Vould you be so hobliging as to favour us with the key?" he continued, addressing Mr. David. who sat sulkily silent. " Hall the same to us, Sir, hall the same. Ve can break down the door, if you vishes."

The grinding sound continued all the while he was speaking, and appeared inexpressibly to exasperate the old man.

A few vigorous charges and kicks from the officer brought down the door, and they perceived before them a narrow flight of stairs which descended to a room, half cellar, half kitchen, lighted by a guttering candle. The Jewess, in her foreign dress, sat beside a small stove, a coffee mill in her lap.

No sooner had the detective espied the stove,

than he sprang forward, upset it, and scattered the coals all over the brick floor. The sound of an outlandish oath came from the top of the stairs. Walter, glancing up, saw the Jew's grey head peering down, his features distorted with rage and fear. The Jewess sat unmoved, watching the party with her bold and haughty stare, behind which glittered a treacherous exultation.

"Give us a poker, somebody, quick," exclaimed the policeman, kicking apart the coals, and looking sharply around him. "The hold rascal 'as been and put it in 'ere."

The Jewess rose. As she moved she knocked down a poker, which rested against the wall behind her. The officer seized it, and raked carefully among the coals. The fire had been but recently kindled, and had been apparently smothered by the premature shutting off of the draught.

"'Ere it is," he exclaimed, triumphantly, drawing forth on the extremity of the poker a smoke-blackened circle.

Mr. Daubenay and Walter stooped over it as he held it to the candle. They saw the outlines of two eagles' heads supporting an empty rim. Walter heard Mr. Daubenay's hurried breathing.

" Hadn't we better go upstairs ? " he asked.

They left the cellar, the Jewess, and the over-turned stove ; and ascended to the room above, where the old Jew was sitting, gnawing his nails.

" Now, Mr. David," said the detective, " you see ve've got it. I could get a varrant and har-rest you in 'alf an 'our if I chose—harest you as a receiver of stolen goods. And that his vot I am going to do." The Jew wrung his hands. " Hunless you tell us this werry minute vere you got the ring; for has to Habraham and Riga, and hall that—it's bosh ! "

The Jew looked wildly about the room.

" Praps you can trust the lady down below to take care of your walluables vile you're gone, for gone you vill be ; praps you vould prefer to leave that remarkably good-looking young 'ooman

in the red silk dressing-gown to take care of herself. I don't vant to meddle vith any gen'l'man's
private concerns. If you vishes it so, it's werry
easily managed. Hall you've got to do is jist to
'old yer tongue, and I'll come vith a nice wan
and carry you avay in style."

The Jew kicked on the ground, then rose, and
struck forcibly on the door.

The detective opened it, and followed him into
another room, the same into which Walter had
been introduced on his first visit. The old man
opened a safe, took out a greasy day-book, and
turned over the pages until he came to an entry,
which he silently pointed out. The officer beckoned
to the gentlemen. They advanced, and bending
over the old man's shoulder, read, deciphering
with difficulty the crabbed characters and distorted spelling of the entry,

"One ring set with orange coloured diamond.
Mrs. Williams. No. 35, Chadlink Street."

The Jew tried to hide the last part of the

entry, but the officer tapped on the back of his hand, and he removed it.

"Paid £65."

"Now, Sir," said the officer, as they left the house, "ve'd best go to the 'ooman's afore this ere David can give her a 'int to get hout of the vay. I'll keep out o' sight. You'd better begin vith a little coaxing—that suits vimmen best; you can get more out o' them that vay, and then there's more chance of vot you do get being true. They'll lie as soon as they're frightened, lie right and left, every vun o' them." And having expressed this rather derogatory opinion of the intrepidity of the feminine mind, the officer turned his attention to the passergers in the streets.

"There goes a precious rascal," he said, pointing out to his companions a large well-dressed man with a fat white face, and a broad brimmed hat, who was carrying a well worn book under his arm. "He's a solicitor of subscriptions for a Horphan Hasylum for the children of Burrum-merapoota, or some sich place as nobody hever 'eard of before; and he makes a pretty leetle business out of it too. He 'ocussed a hold lady hout of a bequest of two thousand puns for it. She died a vhile ago, and the heirs vent to law about it. He got Tangleton, paid him five hundred puns, got the suit, and pocketed the other fifteen hundred. I was in court that day. You should 'ave 'eard the vay Tangleton laid it on to the 'eirs; 'snatching the grains of rice from the starving mouths of the horphans and fatherless, who vere stretching their little brown 'ands 'out for 'elp from the brethren of Christ," that's vot he called it. It set all the other lawyers sniggering, but it made the jury vipe their hies, and got the verdict."

"Why isn't the man taken up?" asked Walter.

"Lord, Sir, if ve vere to take up hall the knaves, the fools vouldn't be hany the better for it; they'd turn hinto hout-and-out hidiots if their vits veren't sharpened hup a leetle that vay now and then. The knaves are a reg'lar Providence for them, Sir."

A view which, though novel to his hearers, was apparently a received doctrine of the officer's.

They stopped at the door of a dingy house, number thirty-five, Chadlink Street. A dirty servant girl opened the door.

" She's gone, Sir, she went a fortnight ago," she answered to Mr. Daubenay's enquiry.

" No, Sir, I don't know where. Perhaps Missis does ;— won't you walk in, gentlemen ?"

And she ushered them into a small, thoroughly-smoked parlour, whose dingy carpet, discoloured paper hangings, and shabby furniture, bespoke it to belong to one of the meanest of so-called respectable lodging houses.

The girl ascended to the story above, whence she promptly returned, looking much dis-composed.

" Missis says, Sir, that she doesn't know nothing about her and she doesn't want to.

That she went as she came, and nobody knows where."

" But, my good girl," said Mr. Daubenay, " it is of great importance to me to find out. Tell your mistress that we beg she will be so good as to speak with us one moment. We will not detain her."

The girl disappeared, but with a face ominous of ill success. The event justified her previsions.

" Missis says, Sir, that she's been worreted enough, and that she won't hear no more about her."

" This is singular," said Walter in a low voice. " It looks as though there were something behind. Had you not better question the girl ?"

Mr. Daubenay put a crown piece into the girl's hand.

" Now be so good as to answer me a few questions, and answer them carefully."

The girl looked deeply impressed, but whether by the sight of the crown piece, or by the earnest tone of Mr. Daubenay's voice, was not so apparent.

"Yes, Sir. I'll tell all as I knows, Sir."

"What sort of person was this Mrs. Williams?"

"She was a very nice sort of a lady, Sir."

"Describe her, if you please."

"She was tallish, and very pale and sickly like, and didn't never go out, hardly."

"Her husband was not here with her?"

"I don't think she had any, Sir. She always wore widow's mourning."

"Did she seem to have any acquaintances?"

"Nobody never came to see her, Sir, while she was here, except a Frenchwoman. She came three or four times. The last time she came was the day before Mrs. Williams went away."

"Do you know the name of the French woman?"

"No, Sir."

"Nor her address?"

"No, Sir."

" What sort of woman was she ?"

" She was short and pretty, and was dressed very fine."

" You are sure you don't know her name ? '

" No, Sir. I only heard her first name once. Mrs. Williams called after her as she went down stairs. It made me think of aniseed tea, I remember; but what it was I can't say."

Mr. Daubenay looked completely bewildered.

" Was it Anaïs ?" asked Walter, who had read French novels.

" Yes, Sir. I think that was it, Sir. It isn't so much like aniseed as I thought it was, but I think that was it, Sir."

" That's one thing gained," said Walter.

The girl slipped the crown into her pocket. She seemed to consider that her last answer entitled her to it, a point on which she had before felt doubtful.

" Did Mrs. Williams appear to have money ?"

" No, Sir; that was the trouble between her and Missis. She got out of what money she had, and though she used to sew and embroider from morning till night and half the night, too, yet she couldn't get along. She had to sell what little jewellery she had. It wasn't much, only two rings and a locket."

"Can you tell me where she disposed of them?"

"Yes, Sir. She had a pearl ring, and a black and gold one. I saw them only a few days ago at Mr. Pritchard's window, the jeweller in the next street, Sir."

"Do you know anything about a ring with a stone of an orange colour?"

"No, Sir."

"Did you ever hear of a Mr. David?"

"No, Sir."

"You are sure?"

"Yes, Sir."

"How did Mrs. Williams go away?"

"She had some trouble with Missis, Sir. She hadn't paid for two or three weeks; the lodgers always pay by the week here, Sir. And Missis was very loud, and Mrs. Williams cried a great deal, and the next morning she got up and went out early, and when she came back she paid Missis and made up her clothes in a bundle, and went away."

" And that is all you know ?"

" Yes, sir."

" I think we had better call in the officer," said Walter.

" Oh, Lor', Sir, I hope you havn't got nothing against me," exclaimed the girl. " As sure as the sun's in the sky, Sir, I've told the truth, all I knows of it, Sir."

Leaving Mr. Daubenay to quiet the girl's apprehensions, Walter summoned the officer.

" Jist tell your missis not to discompose herself, my dear," said the officer to the girl, " but say as how these two genelmen and I vould feel very pertiklerly hobliged if she vould come downstairs for a leettle friendly chat."

In a few moments the mistress of the house appeared. She was a hard, brazen-faced woman, her broad shoulders enveloped in a faded shawl. A dirty cap with flaunting cherry-coloured ribbons was set sideways upon her head ; it formed obviously a recent and hurried addition to her toilette.

" Well, gentlemen, and what do you please to want of me?" she asked angrily, as she flounced into the room.

The officer measured her with his eye for a moment, then advanced.

" Now, ma'am, has you are a person of good sense, you vill perceive that ve shouldn't have come in this vay hexcept on serious bis'ness. The best thing you can do, is to hanswer our questions as far as you are hable, and that vill save you from vot might praps be rather hunpleasant to a lady."

The mixture of indirect menace and implied compliment seemed somewhat to subdue the woman. Mr. Daubenay followed up the impression thus made by laying a sovereign upon the table.

"I do not wish to take up your time unnecessarily," he said.

The woman's face changed suddenly at the sight of the gold. She became fawningly obsequious at once.

"Oh, Sir, it's not that, but a poor lone woman like me, Sir, is so worreted and hustled about, what with people going out and coming in, Sir ;—and what is it that you are pleased to want to know, Sir ?"

"Simply whether you can give us any information respecting a person by the name of Williams, who has been lodging with you."

"I don't know much, Sir. She was a decent sort of body enough, only it was all I could do to get my money out of her. She seemed to have been better off. She could talk French, for I have heard her with a French woman who came two or three times to see her, but she was chary enough of speaking English."

"When did she come ?"

"In the beginning of August, Sir."

" And when did she leave ?"

" A fortnight ago."

" Did she receive any letters while she was here ?"

" No, Sir. The lodgers' letters are always given to me, and she never got any."

" Do you know where she was before she came here ?"

" No, Sir. She came here one day and asked to see the room, and the next day she came in a cab with her trunk."

" Where is that trunk ? She did not take it away, I believe. Perhaps her former address may be on it."

" It was an old worn-out box, Sir, and I think she must have burnt it up for fire wood before she went, for she only took a bundle with her when she went away, and there was no box or anything left in her room. She had sold all the rest of her clothes that was in it, little by little, I expect."

" Thank you, I will not detain you any longer," said Mr. Daubenay.

" I am sorry I can't give you any more satisfaction, Sir," said the woman, following him to the door. "I never thought of anyone's taking an interest in such a poor looking body, else I'd have found out more before she went away."

Mr. Pritchard, the jeweller, in the adjacent street, to whom they next had recourse, perfectly remembered the orange-coloured stone, though he had forgotten its setting. He had declined buying it, as it was not what he wanted. He had given, at Mrs. William's request, the addresses of several dealers, among them that of the Jew. Further than this he knew nothing.

"Now, Sir, the honly thing to do is to hadwertise in the 'Times,'" said the officer, "That is the way to bring her hout. I don't fancy she stole the stone. I think she came by it 'onestly. Ve 'aven't learnt much, but vot ve 'ave learnt goes for and not against her. Hif she did'nt steal it, she vill be glad enough to tell ow she came by it, and get the money."

The advertisement was accordingly sent to the "Times."

CHAPTER V.

It was on Saturday that Walter had returned to the Hall. On Monday evening he roused himself from the depression which had sunk upon him, mounted, and took his way alone to the Park. Perhaps he should hear something of Edith.

As he galloped up to the gates of the Park, a woman shrieked from within the lodge.

" What's the matter there, Joseph ?" he asked, as a man came out and threw open the gate. "Is anyone ill ?"

" No, Sir, thank you, Sir," replied the man in an embarrassed voice. " It's only my old woman, Sir, as was afeard."

"Afraid—afraid of what?" returned young Arden. "Not of me, I hope."

" Oh, no, Sir, not if she'd ha' know'd it. But she thought—" He stopped abruptly.

" Thought what?"

" She thought as how it was Sir Ralph's ghost, Sir."

Walter laughed. The sound rang out on the frosty air an instant, then suddenly ceased. Its echo smote with a painful discord on the young man's ear.

" I tell her so, Sir. I tell her that every-one, gentle and simple, would take her for a natural, to be thinking ghosts rode on horse-back."

The lodge-keeper at the park was a friend of Walter's, he had made many a trout fly for him in former times, and invented for his benefit, and to the great injury of the rabbits, many a snare. Young Arden had often chatted by the hour with him. He knew him to be a man of more than average intelligence, and yet his objections to his wife's apprehensions arose apparently not so much from her believing in the possibility of the apparition of Sir Ralph's spectre, as in that of the impossible phantom of a horse. What could such a belief be supported by? Walter's curiosity was piqued; moreover, he was glad to have his attention distracted a moment from the gnawing heart-ache within.

"Now, Joseph, tell me frankly, do you, such a reasonable fellow as you are, believe in ghosts"?

"Well, Sir, I never used to."

"But do you now?"

"I don't want to, Sir, but I can't help it."

"Did you ever see one?"

"No, Sir, but I've heard one."

"What do you mean? Tell me. I shan't laugh at you."

"Well, Sir, I heard Sir Ralph's ghost twice, the night he was drownded, and my old woman did too, Sir, and that's the reason she's been so scary ever since."

Walter recalled the boy's account of the cry

that had sounded down the river by night.   The
lodge keeper had heard the unfortunate man's
shriek as he fell in.

"I don't see the necessity of supposing any
ghost in the matter.   You heard Sir Ralph's
cry when he fell in."

"Well, Sir, granted I did, when Sir Ralph
was in the river, he couldn't shout in two places
at once, I take it, Sir."

"Certainly not."

"Well, Sir, after that first screech, as I was
lying awake, wondering what on earth such an
awful sound could have come from, I heard
another just like it come from the house, only it
wasn't so loud as the first one, for the house is
further off a long ways, than the river.   And it
was his ghost, Sir, gone to tell them at the house,
Sir.   And there's no disbelieving what one hears
with one's own ears, Sir."

The man's obstinacy was impenetrable.   He
had obviously made up his mind to believe in a
ghost, and believe in it he would.   But what

was that story Edith had repeated about the maids at the park having been wakened by a shriek that same night—a shriek that he had thought must have come from some one in the house that had a nightmare.   It was strange that the lodge keeper should have been able to hear it, and moreover that he should assert it to be the same voice that had sounded from the river. But there was no use in thinking of it.   There had been some coincidence, some dog had chanced to howl, or owl to hoot just at the time.   He was about riding on, when he remembered the woman's shriek at the sound of the horse's hoofs.

"But, Joseph, what had all this to do with the galloping of a horse?"

"Why, Sir, it was just after that first screech that a horse went galloping like mad along the road."

"Kathleen running away after she had thrown Sir Ralph into the river."

"Perhaps it was, Sir, but my old woman puts it altogether, Sir, and when she hears a horse galloping in the night, she thinks a ghost is close by, Sir."

" Well, good evening, Joseph. Tell your wife from me, that Sir Ralph will never come back to frighten anybody."

And Walter rode up the avenue. " A capital site for a ghost story," he said to himself, as he came out from the shadow of the trees, and crossed the lawn on which the horse fronted. He stopped his horse a moment, and looked around him. The sky was almost black. The stars gazed fixedly down upon the long, grey house with its pine bordered terrace, its tall chimneys, its projecting gables and heavy windows As he turned his eye around, it rested on an unformed object crouching beside the house, near the extremity of the terrace. He watched it. It did not move. Could it be some burglar who had stolen there to study the premises, prior to some nocturnal attempt? He threw himself from his horse, and sprang down the terrace. The figure rose to gigantic height, turned the corner, and disappeared. Walter was close behind it. He reached the end of the house, and glanced hastily down the western side. Not an object was in sight.

Very strange. It looked as tall as Goliath, but of course it wasn't he. What could it have been? He stopped before the place where the figure had been crouching. In the dead silence, a faint, distant sound, constantly reiterated, met his ear. He drew nearer and listened. It sounded like a hammering, deep down at the foundations of the wall.

"It puts one in mind of stories about coiners of false money," he thought to himself. "I have often heard such sounds, and never have been able to trace them. It's strange that people stopped at the death-watch, and didn't go on and call these coffin makers."

He returned to the front of the house, and entered. As he was taking off his outer coat, Goliath passed through the hall. He saluted the young gentleman with that smile which is characteristic of his race, an open, frank smile, expressive of a fulness of satisfaction quite impossible to northern physiognomies.

"It could not have been he," thought Walter, "but who then was it?"

Lady Tremyss and Isabel were alone. Lady Tremyss was sitting before a table covered with books and pamphlets. He shook hands with her, and turned towards Isabel, who was seated on a sofa at a little distance, holding Mimi on her lap.

"Why, Mimi, how long it is since I have seen you," he said, as the cat jumped from Isabel's arm, and came rubbing against him.

"Isabel kept her shut up all the time Miss Arden was at the Hall. Miss Arden is afraid of cats," said Lady Tremyss. "I believe Isabel would have shut me up too, had the same cause existed," she added, smiling.

Walter had rarely heard so long a sentence from Lady Tremyss; and her manner was altered, how he knew not, but there was a certain change, —more grace, a greater variety of intonation, a sweeter fall at the end of the phrases, a gentle persuasiveness of accent.

"Oh, Mimi, you must not do that," exclaimed Isabel, as Mimi, after rubbing round Walter, retired to a little distance and began to sharpen her claws upon the carpet.

"You had better carry her away," said Lady Tremyss.

Isabel caught up the animal and took it out of the room.

"I have a favour to ask of you," said Lady Tremyss.

Walter expressed his readiness to obey her every wish.

"Isabel is so depressed by the loss of her friend that I am quite concerned. I did not expect that she would care so much; and I want to try to amuse her, and so I am planning getting up some little vaudevilles, and I want your help; not so much for the acting," she continued, watching Walter's face, "as for general supervision and assistance of that sort. Perhaps I am too *exigeante*, you will think, but I know you better than anyone else, and I think you will not refuse me."

Walter was very much tempted to decline having anything to do with the thing, but a multitude of reasons conspired to force him into acquiescence.

"Your mother has been engaging me," he said to Isabel, as she came back. "What is my post to be?" he added, turning to Lady Tremyss.

"Manager," she answered.

"It's very kind of you, I'm sure," said Isabel.

"The first thing to be decided upon is the play," continued her mother. "I have here an abundance to choose from."

Walter rose and looked them over. Nearly all French.

"What sort of French will your actors speak do you think?" he inquired, with a half smile.

Lady Tremyss was turning over the books. She did not immediately reply.

"They would do very well if they all spoke like Mamma," said Isabel. "My French governess said that she talked the language to perfection. Nothing would convince her that she wasn't a Frenchwoman."

"I must ask Lady Tremyss how you speak," said Walter "I suppose you won't tell me yourself."

"Oh, it's quite natural that I should speak well. I always talked French with Mamma when I was a child, even after we came here."

Lady Tremyss raised her head and shot a glance at Isabel. Isabel's face was turned towards Walter; she did not catch it.

Lady Tremyss bent her head again over the books.

"Strange that it should have been possible in England," returned Walter.

"But we weren't at first in England; we were ever so far off; i'ts so long since I've thought of it, that I can't remember the name. Where was it, Mamma?"

"In Gibraltar," replied Lady Tremyss. "Now,

Isabel, I want Mr. Arden to tell me which of these two plays he thinks the best, ' Le Secret d' Eulalie,' or ' Le Revenant d' Outre Mer.' "

Lady Tremyss' accent was indeed perfect, as Walter perceived from the few words contained in the titles.

" I like the first best," he said, after looking them over. " Our English private performers always fall through when they try tragedy. They are comic against their will."

" Yes, Mamma," said Isabel, " don't you remember when Mrs. Lacy got up private theatricals last year, and Miss Rashton insisted upon acting Adrienne Lecouvreur ;—how every one laughed till they cried, and Mrs. Lacy told her that they cried till they laughed, and she found out the truth from Lady Thorncliffe, and shut herself up, and said she had the headache, and cried herself ill the next day, she was so angry."

" Yes," said Walter. " I was there. I thought it too much of a farce to be laughed at."

" Then it is the ' Secret d' Eulalie,' that we

are to have," said Lady Tremyss. "There are some very amusing situations in it; and there being two heroines, Eulalie and Isabelle, is a great advantage."

" Which part shall you take?" asked Walter, looking at Isabel. " I suppose that of your namesake."

" I don't mean to act," she replied. " If Edith were here I would. I should like to act with her; but as for acting with Miss Calcroft or Miss Wharnbligh, I really couldn't do it. I should hate them for being so unlike her. These heroines are friends, you know."

" You are too romantic, my dear," said Lady Tremyss. " Mr. Arden will think you very extravagant." Lady Tremyss smiled. " She has seen but little of the world, you know," she said to Walter, as if in apology.

Isabel turned her head away; tears were in her eyes.

" How depressed she seems. No wonder her mother wants to amuse her," thought Walter.

" There is one thing for which I must depend upon you," continued Lady Tremyss, " a little serenade that I want you to translate. I will write off the original at once."

" I will do what I can with it," said Walter, " but I've not written verses since I was at school."

" I shall not be hard to please," she answered, while a smile glittered over her features, like a flash of distant lightning.

She drew a portfolio towards her, and began to copy the verses.

" I've had a letter from Edith," said Isabel to Walter.

" Have you ?"

" Yes, and have felt so dull ever since."

" Why ?"

" It makes her seem further away, instead of nearer. She seems so contented, thinking of nothing but her father."

" That is right, is it not ?" asked Waltèr, uttering one of those prodigious falsehoods by implication, into which we are all forced at times.

" I suppose so; but you see I can't bear to have her happy when I am not. I was so happy going over to the Hall, and seeing her every day, and now the time seems so long. I miss my rides with her, and all that, so much, you know."

" Yes. I can imagine how changed—" Walter stopped, then resumed—" You must let me ride with you sometimes; not that I can hope to take her place."

Lady Tremyss raised her head.

" Indeed I wish you would, Mr. Arden. I have sprained my side, and can't go out with her, and she does not care to go alone. It will be only for a day or two."

It was arranged that Walter should call for Isabel the next day.

As Lady Tremyss gave into his hand the copied verses, he rose to take his leave.

" By-the-by, perhaps I ought to tell you that I saw something rather odd as I rode up."

He described the crouching figure, and its inexplicable disappearance.

" It was as tall as Goliath ; but, of course, it could not have been he. Perhaps it would be as well to have a good watch kept to-night. Clapham House was broken into not long ago, you know."

" I have no doubt but that it was Goliath," returned Lady Tremyss. " The house is old, and infested with mice and rats, and I believe he takes them for evil spirits. I have seen him more than once listening in that way."

" Yes," said Isabel. " Edith and I heard them once in the old dancing-room, and we called Mamma, and Mamma called him, and I believe they frightened him so that he has hidden the key, for it has been lost ever since."

" Strange," remarked Walter. " He looks like a man of such resolution."

" I don't think him a coward, in the common sense of the word, but merely timid and superstitious, like all blacks," said Lady Tremyss, leaving her seat, and going towards the fire. The flame sent up a crimson glow over her black dress and statue-like face as she stretched her slender hands towards it.

" Warm yourself well before you go out," she said. " It is cold, very cold." She smiled ex-ultantly.

That smile haunted Walter as he rode down the avenue. He saw Lady Tremyss' face, as she stood on the white marble hearth before the fire, the shadows all inverted by the light from below; the mocking curve of her lip; the fierce gladness in her eye. Why should she rejoice at the biting cold that was chilling him to the bone, even through his furred riding coat? He wondered in vain.

When Walter called at the Park the next day, Isabel was not quite ready. Lady Tremyss received him.

" I am sorry that you are kept waiting; but, now that you are here, I mean to profit by it to ask you to draw me a plan of the fixtures for the curtain and the lights. The carpenter was here this morning; but I found it difficult to make him understand what I wanted. Perhaps you will be so kind."

Walter, who was a good draughtsman, in a few moments executed what was required of him. He sat absently drawing figures upon a blank sheet of paper, while Lady Tremyss examined the sketch he had made.

" That will give a very pretty effect," she said, laying it down. "But what have you here?" she asked, taking up the sheet on which he had been sketching.

As she glanced over it, she started as if struck by a ball. Walter looked quickly up. He beheld only the calm, impassive face he was accustomed to see.

" This branch is very graceful, you should make use of it in a drawing. And this ring setting,—how peculiar it is. Two eagles' heads, is it not? Where did you meet with it?"

" In London," answered Walter, who felt himself bound to secrecy.

" What stone was it set with?" she asked
carelessly, as she laid the sheet upon the
table.

" An orange-coloured diamond," said Walter,
rising to shake hands with Isabel, who entered
at that moment in her riding habit.

" When will you come up again?" said Lady
Tremyss, as he bade her good morning. " You
know that your duties will be onerous. I must
claim much of your time for a week or two; then
I will leave you free."

" I shall have the verses ready by to-morrow ;
To-morrow evening, if you like."

On the next evening he came. He found
Isabel alone, leaning back in an easy chair before
a window whence she had drawn back the cur-
tains. She was pale and serious. He seated
himself near her.

" Are you star-gazing ? " he asked.

" I wish I could read them," she replied ; then,

after a pause, I asked " Do you think that there's any truth in it?"

" No; of course I don't."

" But why should there not be? What wonderful predictions have been made by their aid!" replied Isabel, who, like most persons of lively imagination and undeveloped judgment, had a strong bias towards superstition.

" I don't know of any whose success could not be accounted for on other grounds," answered Walter, looking on her with a good-natured smile, such as we bestow upon the amusing unreason of a little child.

She caught the expression.

" Ah, you think I am foolish," she returned; " but wise men have thought as I do."

" I know it," said Walter; " but they don't think so now-a-days, you know."

" May there not be forgotten truths as well as unknown truths?" asked Isabel, turning her eyes full upon him. " And the unknown is all around us. We cannot put forth our hand without touching it."

An indescribable pain vibrated in her accents.

"Sometimes it is better for us not to know," responded Walter.

He stopped for a moment, then continued,

"But you were asking if there mightn't be forgotten truths. Of course there are; but only when those truths were mixed up with errors which vitiated them. Truth cannot die."

"But we have wandered a good way from our starting point," he resumed, after a pause. "Where can you have studied this science you're talking about?"

"In the book of Ben Houssi of Granada. Did you ever read it?"

"I never heard of it."

"We have a translation of it in the library. I often read it."

"And what have you learned from it?"

"That we must all fulfil our fate, and that our fate is written there."

She glanced at the stars.

"Then past fate must be written there also. The stars do not change, you know."

Isabel looked up earnestly.

" How I wish —"

" Wish what ? "

" That I could read about Mamma," she answered, almost in a whisper.

" Do you want to know what is going to happen to her ? "

" Not so much that." She hesitated a little, then seeming to yield to some urgent impulse, continued, speaking more rapidly, " I want to know what has befallen her already. I want to know all about her. I feel so lonely sometimes. I did not use to think about it or care ; but now I wish she would talk to me, and tell me all about her past."

There was a mournful tone to the girl's voice that moved Walter. In truth were this so, what a lonely life Isabel's must be. How sad the isolation that she described.

He sat silent an instant, then said,

" It is not unnatural that she shrinks from looking back. You know that your father's death—"

"Yes, I know," answered Isabel; "but—"
And she seemed to carry on her thoughts silently.
Walter looked at her attentively.

"You are tired, I fear. Did I take you too far
yesterday?"

"Oh, no; it is not that. If I am a little
tired, it is because I had such a disturbed night.
I am sure Mamma is working too hard at that
translation. She talked in her sleep a great deal.
The door between her room and mine is always
open at night, and she kept me awake. She was
talking to one of the characters, Mrs. Williams,
half the night, and begging her to hide her so
that nobody could find her and take her away."

"Mrs. Williams!" ejaculated young Arden.

"Yes. When I told her of it this morning,
she did not remember anything about it; but she
said she had changed the names of the people
from French to English, and that Madame
Duvernay she had altered to Mrs. Williams, and
that she must have been dreaming about that.
But here she is."

Lady Tremyss came into the room with a roll of paper in her hand.

"I have been busy, you see," she said, unfolding the sheets as she seated herself by the lamp.

"Have you done all that to-day?" he asked.

"No, I began it yesterday." She turned to the table.

"May I see it?"

He took the sheets which she held out, and looked over the list of *dramatis personæ*. There was the name, "Mrs. Williams." He glanced at her anew. He might as well have scrutinized an iron mask. The beautiful features rested immoveable in the lamplight. His look sought in vain to penetrate her eyes. It was stopped just below the surface as by an adamantine wall. He looked back to the paper, 'Eugenie,' 'Adeline.' "I thought the names were Eulalie and Isabel. I must re-write my translation."

"First let me see it," she said.

Walter drew a folded sheet from his pocket book.

"This is far better than the original. 1 am much obliged to you. I shall show it to all my friends," said Lady Tremyss.

"Indeed, I must beg that you will not," said Walter, quickly, "as it was to be sung, I thought no one would pay any attention to the words. I am not at all satisfied with it."

"Very well, since you request it, I will keep it secret. Mind, Isabel, that you tell no one, not even Miss Arden. But it is not at all worth while to re-write it merely because of the change of name."

She carefully locked the paper in her desk.

"Now we must decide whom we are to ask to fill the parts. There is a gay widow—I think of Mrs. Lacy for her; and a lively young lady whose part Isabel ought to take; and a quiet young lady, for whom Miss Wharnbligh would do very well."

"And the men, Mamma?" asked Isabel. "It will be much harder to find the men."

"There is a sporting young gentlemen,—Mr.

Renson would scarcely need to study the part; a student, for whom we must find as much of a book-worm as possible; a guardian—"

" A cross guardian ?" enquired Isabel.

" No, an amiable guardian, quite in the style of Mr. Tracy; and a wicked cousin, for whom we must choose some remarkably good young man."

" Why so ?" asked Walter.

" No one else would take the part."

" Then Mr. Milcum will do," said Isabel. " I know he would take it if I asked him."

" I have no doubt he would," observed Walter, whose principal remembrance of Mr. Milcum was that of seeing him on a tall black horse, trying in vain to keep up with Isabel; who, ably seconded by Moira, was maliciously leading him through a dangerous bog, under pretence of shewing him one of her favourite points of view.

The conversation turned upon the several merits of the performers proposed; others were suggested, canvassed, and finally rejected; and when Walter took his leave, matters were not much further advanced than they were before; except that it was decided that he should see Mr. Renson the next day, and ride over in the evening and report his answer.

So the preparations and arrangements went on day after day. At the end of the second week Walter had been every evening at the Park, and as yet Miss Wharnbligh had not made up her mind, so in consequence nothing had been settled.

Walter's time was entirely taken up by the multifarious responsibilities which pressed upon him. It required as much time and management to gather together the materials for a troupe, as to construct a Cabinet when the two sides of the House are evenly balanced.

The multiplied and never-ending annoyances which arose day by day were borne by Lady Tremyss, however, with an equanimity most edifying to behold; Isabel's spirits seemed to improve; Walter, though wearied out with the whole matter, yet felt himself bound to go on with it; and Edith, sitting in her blue and grey room at Arden Court, read Isabel's constant letters,—sent, by her mother's advice, in the form of a diary,—followed Walter in his daily visits to the Park, pictured him absorbed in the projected gaiety, and could not refuse to see how entirely he seemed bound to the service of Isabel. She had hoped to find consolation in devoting herself to her father, but that expectation had been defeated. Her mind and character had developed like her body. She had new wishes, new thoughts, new aspirations; and to all these her father was blind, and deaf, and cold. She looked upon him with new eyes. The mantle of habit had been rent away; nor did its folds close again over his foibles and faults. He loved her, but his pervading selfishness tainted even his love, as she felt with unspeakable sadness. She strove in vain for a time to close her eyes against her new perceptions; she blamed herself, accused herself of coldness, ingratitude, irreverence; she recalled the many instances of his affection, his anxiety for her well-being; but she struggled in vain: the balance would right itself, no matter how strongly her will might weigh it down. By an immutable law, the superior character recognized its own superiority ; and Edith was slowly and sorrowfully compelled to acknowledge to herself that her father was other than what she had thought him to be.

So the days went on. She read good books, she worked for the poor, she devoted herself none the less conscientiously to her father, and she grew paler day by day, and week by week, until one morning a letter came which blanched her cheeks so that they could grow pale no longer.

The envelope was directed in Lady Tremyss hand. Within was a copy of verses in Walter's writing.

I lie beside the half heard, murmuring stream,
    And watch the white wreaths on the dark blue sky;
Circling in ceaseless sweep they trace thy name,
    It fills the whole broad heaven to mine eye,
            Isabel.

I seek the quiet of the solemn woods,
  To lose me far from sight and sound of men ;
Thy name runs whispering on from leaf to leaf,
  It fills the silence of each forest glen,
      Isabel.

I wander forth beneath the roof of night;
  Writ there in characters of trembling flame,
Soft quivering through the purple darkness, still
  I see, for ever see, oh love, thy name,
      Isabel.

There was a ringing sound in Edith's ears as she finished; the outlines of the objects around grew dim. When her thoughts cleared again she was lying on the floor. Her consciousness of misery seemed not to have been obscured by the sudden giving way of her physical forces, she awoke to full perception. The blow had been so overwhelming that at first she could not rally. She did not know how she had clung to hope till now that all hope was wrenched from her.

Again she read the verses, shaking in every limb as she did so. There was no possibility of mistake. Walter loved Isabel. She did not care to discover by what accident the lines had come into her own possession. It did not interest her to know. Her mind was filled with her misery ; it had room for nothing else.

The hours passed unheeded as she sat, scarcely conscious of anything, deadened with pain. At last the sun sank. Habit reasserted its power. She remembered that she must dress for dinner ; that her father would soon return. She went up-stairs to her room.

" Dieu ! que Mademoiselle est pâle," exclaimed Félicie. " Mademoiselle est souffrante."

The maid rolled a berceuse to the fire, and gently slipping a pillow beneath Edith's head, removed the comb from her mistress's hair, and loosening her long curls, began silently to bathe her temples with aromatic water.

Félicie, that marvel of the nineteenth century, a Parisian not devoid of heart, had in the short space of time she had been in Edith's service, become attached to her ; and so it was with a gentle, compassionate touch, and in considerate silence, that she performed her office.

The sympathy, blind and narrow as it was, brought yet a tinge of consolation with it. It lessened that first bewildering sense of utter isolation. Edith raised her eyes gratefully to her maid as she thanked her, and rising, moved towards the toilette table.

"Mais, Mademoiselle ne pense pas à se faire habiller!" exclaimed Félicie. "Mademoiselle est blanche comme une linge. Mademoiselle fera mieux de se mettre au lit et de loire une infusion de tilleul. C'est cela qui fera du bien à Mademoiselle : ça calme."

But Edith was regardless of Félicie's exhortations, and she made her toilet as usual. As she was about to leave the room the maid said—

"I had something that I wanted to show to Mademoiselle ; not only because it is so pretty, but because if Mademoiselle would buy it, that would be a veritable act of charity."

Opening a flat box, she displayed a handkerchief, wrought with exquisite skill.

" It is beautiful ; but how is it an act of charity to buy it? Is the workwoman in distress ?"

" I am going to tell it to Mademoiselle. My sister is première demoiselle to try on at Madame Julie's, in Regent Street, and she knew Madame Guillaume, who is not an ouvrière, but used to be a lady, and was very kind to her when in Malta, when Anaïs had the fever coming from Rome with her mistress, and was so ill that they had to leave her at Malta, and Madame Guillaume was so good to her, and nursed her so well. And when she came to London a little while ago her husband had died, and she had no money and no friends, and she had old debts to pay, and so she has to work, and Anaïs sells her work in the shop, and she could sell this for two guineas and a half; but when she showed it to me I told her I would take it home, and that I would make Mademoiselle see it, and Mademoiselle has si bon cœur that perhaps she would give more for it than the shop price."

Edith gave five guineas for the handkerchief, to Félicie's great delight; and charging that p. rsonage to obtain from her sister Madame Guillaume's address, that she might give her an order with which she had been entrusted by Isabel, she went down to meet her father.

Mr. Arden had been more occupied with business since Edith's return than she had ever known him before. He returned late from the city, and often spent the evening in writing. She had fancied that he seemed anxious as well as pre-occupied. But on this evening all that harassed him appeared to have cleared away ; he was in high good humour, and much more jocose than was his wont. It was a cumbrous sort of gaiety, not quite to Edith's taste, although she did her utmost to smile and respond to it.

" You have been living like a nun since you returned," he said, as the dinner at length ended, he sat in the library over his cup of coffee, " Now I must make you amends." And deaf to Edith's protestations that she liked living quietly, and did not want any company, he began to lay plans for a series of entertainments, at the prospect of which Edith's courage well-nigh failed her. A sensation of desperation came over her as she listened.—How was she to endure all this? Why was her father so anxious for her to see company? What good did he hope to obtain?—His next words told her.

"I was speaking about it to Lady Charlotte Estbridge just before you came back. She talked very well. She said that a girl's success depends more on what is said of her before she's out, than most people think; and that she had known many a young woman fail, simply because people didn't know that they were expected to admire her. She has consented to be your *chaperone* next season. I think I have done very well to secure her."

Mr. Arden did not think it necessary to mention that it had been a business transaction, certain of Lady Charlotte's depreciated shares of the ———— Railway having been purchased by him of her man of business, at par, as a preliminary to his request.

"But, Papa, I don't care to be admired," said Edith, raising her eyes mournfully. "It won't make me any happier."

"If you are so very unlike other girls as not to care for your own success, I do. A great deal depends on it," he responded, brusquely.

"What depends on it, Papa? I don't see that we want anything," glancing around the sumptuous apartment.

Her father knit his brows. The memory of the nameless affronts, the petty insults, the veiled but biting sarcasm which had met him in his upward path, rose freshly within him at her words. He knew himself to hold his social position merely because of his wealth. He felt a galling consciousness that he enjoyed no personal consideration whatever. He had determined to ally himself strongly, to attach to his interest some noble name. And it was as much for her good as for his own so to do. People might say what they pleased, wealth was not omnipotent—some people could not be bought. There was no need of talking to Edith. When the occasion presented itself, then it would be time enough to press the point.

He looked at her as she sat in profile, her hands folded on her knee, her eyes fixed on the hearth. How pale and listless she appeared. He hoped her health was not going to fail again. His affection for her, selfish though he was, rose uppermost for the moment.

"Why, my pet, you are not looking so well as I would like," he said caressingly.

Edith drew her chair nearer, and put her hand into his.

"Is anything the matter?"

"Nothing, Papa."

"Is there anything you wish for?"

"No, Papa."

A renewed suspicion crossed his mind, and brought with it an impatient resolution to find out the truth at once.

" Do you want to go back to the Hall? "

" No," she answered, with sudden vehemence. " Anything but that."

We are occasionally more perplexed by answers to our queries than we were by the uncertainties which led to our questions. Mr. Arden found himself in that condition. He had thought a while before that Edith had rather a liking for her cousin, and now here she was passionately protesting her dislike of the Hall. He didn't understand it. However, one thing seemed clear, there was no danger to be apprehended from that quarter. He had been needlessly alarmed. Perhaps it would have been as well to have given her the letter after all. And yet,—no, it was safer as it was.

Edith slept late on the ensuing morning. When she awoke her father was gone to the City, and a letter was waiting for her, a second note directed in Lady Tremyss' handwriting. Within were a note from Isabel, and a few lines from Lady Tremyss, wherein she explained that she

had offered the day before to enclose and direct
the accompanying note, Isabel having been called
away, and that she had taken another sheet by
mistake. She begged Edith to send back the
enclosure of the day before by return of mail,
requesting her to speak of it to no one, and to
write to Isabel as if she had not seen it. "Mr.
Arden desires that it should not be known," the
note concluded, "and I have promised him to
keep it secret."

Edith re-enclosed the lines. She added a brief
note.

"DEAR LADY TREMYSS,

"Your wishes shall be complied with.

"Ever yours truly,

"EDITH ARDEN."

That done, she set herself resolutely to work on
a *vide poche* which she had begun for Isabel. She
had nerved herself to endurance. She worked on
with a steady, mechanical motion till she was

interrupted by the announcement of a visitor, Mrs. Lacy, who appeared in her purple dress and bonnet, her long white camel's hair shawl, all border, and her small sable muff, looking exceedingly as if she had stepped in on her way to the Park.

"You see I was not discouraged by finding you out when I called at the Hall," she said, smiling on Edith and on everything about her at once. "You ran away from me, but I have followed you, you see. I am staying a few days at Woodthorpe, quite near you. What a perfect room this is," she continued, ensconcing herself in an easy chair, and gazing complacently around. "I shall be fairly jealous of it."

"Nothing could be prettier than the room you were in at Houston Lacy," replied Edith, who felt a certain liking for Mrs. Lacy, as no one could help doing, despite her endless list of faults.

"Ormanby is always abusing it, and he had almost got me out of conceit with it. But then he is never pleased with anything, you know." .

" Perhaps there is a little of the *métier* in his disapprobation," said Edith, quietly.

" Ah, how ?" asked Mrs. Lacy, turning her eyes full upon her.   She was not used to hear her brother spoken of so coldly.

" I fancied from something he said that he piques himself on liking nothing."

" I dare say.   He has been completely spoilt, as I tell him," responded Mrs. Lacy, in an aggrieved tone, caused by the remembrance of the way in which her brother had taken leave of her and of her guests a few days previously.   " But I come upon business as well as upon pleasure, and I am forgetting all about it.   I want to ask you a great favour."

Edith expressed general willingness to oblige Mrs. Lacy

" It is about Félicie."

" I hope you don't want her back."

" She would not come if I did; but she is the only person who ever dressed my hair to suit me, and I want to know if you could be so kind as to let me send over my maid to learn her way. I have come up for four days, and that would give her quite time enough.

Edith assented.

" I suppose you hear constantly from the Hall."

" Not very often. Mrs. Arden is not fond of letter writing."

" We are quite gay at Wodeton, you know, for a wonder. You have heard of the theatricals at the Park, of course."

" Yes."

" I have come up to order my dress. It will be charming. I am to be a gay widow."

" So I hear."

" I fancy that the play will end in a marriage."

" Most plays do, I think."

" Oh, but I mean a true marriage."

" Indeed."

" Yes. Everyone is talking of it. It must be delightful to you, so fond of her as you were ; and a match very gratifying to Lady Tremyss, I imagine, it keeps her daughter so near her."

" She is very much attached to her daughter,"
said Edith, pressing her hands tightly together.

" Yet how different they are. I must say that
I should not have liked Lady Tremyss for a
mother. I have never got over the feeling she
gave me the night I first saw her. It was at the
opera, just at the last, when somebody was being
killed—I always look away, I hate such things —
and I caught sight of Lady Tremyss's face. It
was frightful to look at, beautiful as she was."

" I have only seen her as the most devoted of
mothers to Isabel; and she has been more than
kind to me."

Edith paused.

" Yes, I know," replied Mrs. Lacy, a little
hurriedly. " That was a noble thing, really
heroic. But then you know first impressions are
strong, though I dare say they often make us
unjust."

The conversation turned a while on indifferent
subjects, and then Mrs. Lacy took her leave.

CHAPTER VI.

WHEN Mr. Arden entered his drawing-room that evening, it was with an air of irrepressible satisfaction. He kissed Edith, then stood before the fire awhile, slowly rubbing his hands together as if enjoying in silence some pleasurable subject of thought.

It was not Edith's practice to question her father, and on this, as on other occasions, she waited for him to speak. He turned at length towards her, and said in a tone which he vainly endeavoured to render careless,

" Well, my dear, I suppose you will be ready by next Tuesday."

" Ready for what, papa?"

"Albansea Castle. I had a note from the Duchess this morning inviting us for a fortnight, and I have accepted."

"There is nothing to be done, papa. I have everything I need."

Mr. Arden looked discontented. He would much rather that Edith had demanded three new dresses for every day, as if she had been going to Compiégne.

"I will see your maid about it, my dear. I wish you to appear well, of course. It is a very distinguished party. I saw Colonel Dive to-day, and he told me who would be there ; Lady Masterton, and Lady Sophia, Lord and Lady Melby, Prince and Princess Wosocki, General and Lady Emmeline Horsmantle, Miss Tellinghurst, Ormanby Averil, Lord Skeffington, Lord Prudhoe, Sir Frances Lister, and one or two others. It will be very pleasant."

Mr. Arden's face shone complacently.

"I don't know anyone except the Duchess and Lord Skeffington," replied Edith, apparently finding the prospect less agreeable than did her father.

"And Mr. Averil."

" I scarcely spoke to him," she answered, in a tone which sufficiently implied dislike.

" I hope, my dear, that you will not allow any unfounded prejudice to render your manners disagreeable towards a gentleman for whom I have great esteem."

Edith looked at him enquiringly.

" I mean Mr. Averil. I particularly desire that you should treat him with politeness."

" Am I ever rude, Papa?" she asked, somewhat astonished by the implied accusation.

" No, my dear, I hope not, but you are very cold. It is not unadvisable to have a certain hauteur to people in general, it looks well; but it is out of place towards such a person as Mr. Averil. You understand me. I wish to be on good terms with him, and that I cannot be unless you are so too," said Mr. Arden, in conclusion, leaving Edith much perplexed at the novel position of importance assigned to her by her father, yet determined to second his wishes as far as possible.

"But how can I ever try to please that man!" she thought to herself again and again during the evening.

The next morning was signalized by a battle royal between Mr. John Arden and Félicie, if such an expression be applicable to a contest where all the forces were superior on the side of the weaker party. He had required the presence of Edith's maid in the library after his breakfast. Félicie entered, courtesied, and stood by the door waiting to learn his pleasure. Félicie had already twice seen her employer, and being of a sharp, discriminating turn of mind, had, during those two brief glimpses, sounded, weighed, and judged him, coming to certain conclusions not altogether complimentary to the pompous gentleman who now stood on the hearth-rug with his back to the fire, warming himself preparatory to his departure.

Contrary to his expectations, Félicie did not seem at all oppressed by the honour he considered he had done her by summoning her to a conference. On the contrary he began to feel himself incommoded by the keen glance with which she stood eyeing him.

" I have sent for you because I wish to speak to you," he said at length, in a magisterial kind of tone, calculated as he fancied to bring the Frenchwoman to fitting sense of his own personal importance.

" E'es, Sare," responded Félicie, audibly, inwardly adding, " Je le savais déjà."

" Your young lady is going to pay a visit."

" E'es, Sare." " Mais allons donc," to herself.

" And I want to know if there be anything she wants."

" For how long time sall Mademoiselle be gone, Sare ?"

" For a fortnight."

' Sall Mademoiselle be en toilette of Eenglish demoiselle, or of French demoiselle ?"

Mr. Arden hesitated, not thoroughly appreciating the difference involved. He thought it best to say French.

" Den, Sare, Mademoiselle do need some evening's dresses, tree or four, and morning's dresses as mush."

" 1 will order them to-day, then."

" Vat, Sare?"

Mr. Arden bent his brows portentously. There was a latent rebellion in the Frenchwoman's tone that must be suppressed at once.

" I said I would order them to-day."

Félicie's eyes shot fire.

"Has Monsieur de habit to command de dresses of Mademoiselle ?"

" Certainly," with an imposing glance.

Félicie's indignation exploded, mindless of Mr. Arden's angry glare.

" Den, Sare, I ave de need to tell you dat you not comprehend de leetlest ting of vat Mademoiselle should vear. Mademoiselle is svelte, and blonde, and angélique in style, and de dresses

she ave in her armoires are all écrasantes. Dey
would be ver well for fat and brune old lady; but
for Mademoiselle dey not de ting. For dat it
require un talent apart, and it is not in de attri-
butes of gentlemans to know vat young demoiselles
should vear."

Mr. Arden was more than a little disconcerted
by this volubly delivered tirade. He perceived that
the Frenchwoman was in no wise afraid of him.
He thought it expedient to temporize.

"I have always ordered them of Madame
Deschamps, and with no regard to cost."

There was an implied apology in the reply
which Félicie was quick to perceive, and take advantage of.

"Madame Deschamps!" she ejaculated, with
an accent of scarcely veiled contempt. "Et
Monsieur a voulu que Mademoiselle soit habillée
chez Madame Deschamps, she who dress all the
douairières de Londres, and who make pay her
dresses by de veight!"

"They always looked very rich," answered Mr.

Arden, who was beginning mentally to look about him for means of retreat.

"Dieu de Dieu!" muttered Félicie. "Est il donc bête, ce gros Monsieur! I ave de honour to inform Monsieur dat Mademoiselle can *not* be dress riche. She must be dress simple, distingué, elégante, but for to dress her riche, nevare. It is a chose inouïe, un vrai raffinement de mauvais goût to dress a jeune demoiselle riche."

"What should she wear?" asked Mr. Arden, vanquished by the authoritative tone of the soubrette.

"She sall vear no flounce, no ruffle, no lace, no nossing as is for dame mariée. She sall vear robes fraiches, couleurs clairs, nuances tendres, tout-à-fait jeune fille; and she sall vear no parures, not von sing sall she put on of bijouterie. No von ave understand Mademoiselle's genre de beauté. I vill make her so dat every von who see her sall say—' C'est un miracle de beauté et de bon goût.' It is so dat I understand it."

Félicie folded her hands before her, and

eyed her master with the air of a general delivering his orders to an aide-de-camp.

Mr. Arden, who dared risk no further encounter, being by this time effectually cowed, considered it expedient to end the interview by conferring upon Félicie unlimited powers as to taste and expense, only exacting that her young lady should be the best dressed of all the young ladies who were to be at Albansea.

Much as Mr. John Arden pondered, he could not arrive at the solution of so unexpected a phenomenon as the arrival of the invitation to Albansea Castle. True, the Duchess frequently honoured his balls and dinner parties with her presence, and invited him to balls and dinner parties in return; but' he had never before been invited to stay even three days at the Castle when it was the fullest; and now that the Duchess, who was in mourning, had but a comparatively small circle about her, (an invitation being consequently far more of a compliment), here he was, with Edith, invited to pass a fortnight.

His perplexities would have been dissipated could he have overheard a conversation which took place between the Duchess and Ormanby Averil, the day on which the invitation was dated.

"Averil," said the Duke, a fat, good natured man, coming into the billiard-room, where Averil stood watching the play between Maurice Westwood and Frank Prinne. "Averil, won't you go to the Duchess? She wants you; something has gone wrong, I believe.—Well done, Westwood," as a sharp double rap was heard. And the Duke took Averil's place, while the latter betook himself to the Duchess.

"Oh, Mr. Averil, I am so annoyed. There was never anything so provoking. Do sit down, and advise me what to do," said that lady, greeting his entrance in a manner that proclaimed him what he was, l'ami de la maison.

"First I must know what your Grace wishes to be advised about," he replied, seating himself near the tall, thin, fair-haired woman who had called him to her aid.

" Here is a note from Miss Telfrey, saying that her grandfather is so ill,—he is really dying, you know, poor old man—that she can't come. I always have a beauty, I have never failed; and here I am left without one. The party will be spoilt."

" But Miss Telfrey is not the only pretty girl," replied Averil, apparently unconvinced of the magnitude of the disaster, and inclined to look upon it more slightingly than suited the Duchess.

·" But she is the only available one," responded that lady in an aggrieved tone. " I don't want a girl whom everyone has seen. I want something new. I always have had it, and I must have it now. And I can't think of any one Now tell me, what am I to do ?"

Averil pondered awhile.

" There is Sophy Marginford ; she is pretty, very, though she is too tall."

" I don't want her, she is not to my taste. That foolish Aunt of hers has turned her head already."

"There never was much weight to balance it.—
Lady Emmeline Forrest."

" She would do, but she's at Witherspee."

" Have you thought of Harriet Bywell?"

" She is stupid. I must have a clever girl—
one that can talk, when the party is to be so
small."

" Then if I understand aright, your requisites
are beauty, novelty, and intelligence."

"Yes, and now I think you must perceive
what a difficulty I am in. Where am I to find
them ?"

"Let me see," he answered, speaking slowly.
" I saw some one at Houston Lacy, a girl not
yet out—a positive beauty, blonde"—he glanced
at the Duchess's yellow curls; he had a point to
carry—" lady-like and clever."

" But if I don't know her—" objected the
hostess.

" I think you have seen her. You know her
father, John Arden."

The Duchess pursed up her lips and sat contemplating the carved ivory handle of the paper knife she was holding. She did not want to ask John Arden, but she had seen the girl at Arden Court, and been pleased with her. She was not so handsome then as Averil described her, but girls alter fast, and she could trust his taste. Yet she really could not make up her mind to ask John Arden ; what was she to do ?"

" What a pity that I can't ask her without her father," she said, regretfully.

" Yes, but I don't think you can."

She sat weighing the matter. How provoking that Miss Telfrey could not come. It was very difficult to make up her mind about it. She would not decide at all. She would leave it to Averil.

" Now tell me, if you were I, what would you do ? It shall be as you say."

" Ask them."

CHAPTER VII.

The country around Albansea was not remarkable for beauty; in fact, as Edith approached the castle, her eyes rested on a wilderness. On either side of the carriage she saw a bleak, desolate plain, over which the sea wind wandered, Before her on a rugged eminence, overhanging the leaden waves which came rolling in from the German Ocean, rose the gray front of the castle, flanked by two enormous round towers, with narrow loopholes and battlemented tops. The dark mass of the building stood out from a background of heavy, white-edged clouds, which rose sullenly from the far distance of the sea.

As Edith gazed upon the frowning pile which

she was rapidly nearing, her heart sank within her. She felt that she might be even more unhappy than she was now. That strange uneasiness which steals over the strongest and least apprehensive amongst us at times, and which may always, when looked back upon, be found to have heralded some crisis in our fate, invaded her mind. She turned her eyes imploringly on her father, as if seeking refuge from some vaguely perceived danger. His face was averted; he was looking intently towards the Castle.

"See, Edith, here comes a riding party—two ladies and three gentlemen. How fast they come on. Ah! this one on the chestnut horse is Ormanby Averil. How well he sits. Look up and bow to him, my love."

Edith looked up. She saw the cold, regular features of Ormanby Averil, and bowed in reply to his salutation; then sank back shivering as the party passed. She felt cold, even beneath her sable cloak and robe.

"Ah, you will soon be comfortably at the Castle, we are not ten minutes from it," said Mr. John Arden, as with his most affectionate look he folded her wrappings more closely around her. "Now, my pet, I shall hope to see a little more colour in your cheeks, and hear a laugh now and then. You have been dull, very dull, at the Court, lately. I was busy, and did not do enough to amuse you. I had much to think of just then." His face took an expression of retrospective anxiety for a moment, but it cleared again as he added, "Now I am quite at liberty, and I hope to see my little girl enjoy herself. Very opportune this invitation. I would rather your first visit should be at Albansea than anywhere else."

His face beamed with satisfaction as the carriage crossed the bridge over the dried-up moat—in summer a flower-garden – belting the fortress, and rolled into the courtyard.

After her reception by the Duchess, Edith was ushered upstairs to her room.

" Dieu, Mademoiselle, que c'est un vrai roman, cette chambre!" exclaimed Félicie, as Edith entered. " Il me semble que je dois habiller Mademoiselle à la Reine Isabeau, tout de suite. Les toilettes modernes n'ont point de rapport avec tout ceci."

The room offered an aspect which gave a colour of reason to Félicie's remarks. It was one of the oldest apartments of the castle, and had been assigned to Edith by the Duchess's command, from a motive which she would not have cared to analyze, but which, if laid open, would have been found to have sprung from a desire to display to the eyes of the daughter of the modern millionaire something which money could not buy.

The walls and vaulted ceiling were lined with blue leather, whereon were stamped ivy leaves of gold. The bed was of satin, embroidered with curious needlework. Great coffers of carved oak, black with age, were placed on either side of the one narrow window; the toilette glass was mounted in ivory yellow with age. Ancient silver candlesticks were placed on the toilet table, and from the centre of the vaulted ceiling hung a silver lamp, of corresponding age and style. The cumbrous chairs were of ebony, cushioned with damask. The floor was covered with a carpet woven to imitate dried rushes mingled with crimson autumn leaves.

There was something bewildering in the consistent antiquity of the apartment. Edith closed her eyes as she leaned back in the great armchair that Félicie placed before the fire, and tried to recover her sense of time and place. She thought of Walter. All her consciousness rushed back in a flood. No need for anything else. She was Edith Arden, come to pay a visit at Albansea. She rose with that restless desire for motion that a sudden stab of pain, mental or bodily, always brings with it, and walking to the window, looked forth upon the sea.

The great waves came rolling up to the shore, driven before the wind. She stood and watched them. She would have turned from a summer landscape, with its glad fields and smiling sky, but in the stern scene before her she found a strange delight. The pain within seemed dulling as she gazed on the rising and falling of the waves. So—and so—and so—for ever—ever rising, ever falling, sweeping on unceasingly, rushing without stay. And thus they would rush, when she was gone, when all who were living were gone ; sweeping, rushing on for ever. Her reverie was broken by her father's knock at the door. Félicie hastily arranged her toilette, and Edith descended.

Averil had thought often of Edith since he had seen her. Her singular and delicate beauty, contrasting with her keen penetration and incisive speech, had given him a sensation to which he had long been a stranger. The quiet sarcasm of her manner had galled him at the moment, the searching glance of her eye had made him uneasy whilst it rested upon him ; yet when she was gone, he recalled sarcasm and glance with something like pleasure. They were so different from what he was used to meeting. It seemed to brace him to remember them.

He had been abominably cross, as Mrs. Lacy assured him, all the day after an unsuc-cessful call at Arden Hall, and he had even con-templated going to town and putting himself in John Arden's way, in order to get another of those invitations to the Court which he had for-merly, as a matter of course, rejected. But an urgent letter from the Duchess had interfered with the execution of this half-formed project, by calling him to Albansea ten days earlier than he expected. And now that the invitation had been sent and accepted, he found himself awaiting Edith's arrival with an impatience which brought back to him some of the long-forgotten memories of his youth.

" A very fine-looking man, mais il lui manque l'air noble. But what a lovely creature that is with him. Who are they ? " said the Princess

Wosocki, a young woman of twenty-six, married to a man of seventy, as John Arden and his daughter entered the room.

"Mr. John Arden, a millionaire, and his daughter," replied Averil, turning so as to watch the quiet grace with which Edith made her *entrée*.

"I like her, she has ideas, I read it in her face," said the Russian, "but she is cold, colder than our snows."

"Then you think her devoid of sentiment?" inquired Averil, who had, and justly, a high opinion of Princess Wara's penetration.

"Did I say that?" she returned, quickly.

"I said she was cold, and so she is cold to all but two or three. But look at her eyes, there is fire in the centre, though they are so soft. When you see an eye like that, clear and profound, soft, with one ray of light steady in the darkness of the middle, then you see one capable of *une grande passion*, a woman who will love, and only love once."

The Princess's light blue eyes expanded as she

gazed at Edith ; her strongly accented, somewhat Cossack features, were instinct with intelligence ; she was obviously speaking *avec connaissance de cause.*

" I have heard you say that in looking at a new face you aim at detecting the strongest and the weakest points of a character, and that, these once ascertained, the rest follows of course," said Averil, after a pause, during which he had been watching Edith.

" Precisely, that is what I do when I find anything worth the while," she replied.

" I fancy, however, that such a rule could scarcely apply to so undeveloped a character as that of a girl of seventeen," he continued, carelessly.

" You call that character undeveloped ? I do not know what you can mean. That young girl has as much strength as either you or I. I am not sure that she has not more."

" Then the two points are discoverable ?"

" Most certainly they are."

"I know your insight is wonderful. I am going to put it to the proof. What is the strongest and what the weakest point of Miss Arden's character?"

The Russian turned her eyes upon him with an enquiring glance. He met it gravely, impassively.

"I do not like such questions," she replied, "but since you ask me, I will tell you what I think."

She inclined her head and watched Edith from under her prominent, oblique eyebrows.

"If she were a Catholic she would be dévote, very likely make herself a nun," she said, as if speaking to herself; then raising her head she answered, "they are one,—self sacrifice."

"How do you know?" asked Averil, scanning Edith's features.

"It is written on her face; besides, it belongs to the type. I do not often see a young girl like that. I shall ask the Duchess to present her."

Before many moments Edith was engaged in

conversation with the Russian, while Averil stood talking to her father, to that gentleman's great gratification.

In the general move to lunch, Averil approached Edith, to whom, as yet, he had only bowed.

"I am happy to meet you again. You left the Hall quite unexpectedly, I believe."

"Quite so."

—Yes, there was the same cold intonation, the same level inclination of the eyebrows, the same quiet hauteur of manner. They were as pleasant as ice in summer.—

Mr. Arden's admonitions had been of no avail. Edith could not be other than chill to people whom she did not like. Averil saw that he did not please her. It was an attraction the more. He took his place beside her at table, and tried to draw her into conversation. He asked of her journey, spoke of the weather, touched on various topics, and was met everywhere by the same courteous, distant reserve. He betook himself to studying the beauty of her little ear, perfectly modelled, but almost too transparent. She wore no ear-rings,—he was glad of that. She was dressed with peculiar simplicity,—that was in good taste. She scarcely tasted anything,—he detested to see a woman with a good appetite. But he must say something.

"It will not be gay here at all, I am sorry to say."

"I am glad," replied Edith, with a look of relief.

" Really !"

A tinge of his accustomed sarcasm was in his tone.

She did not answer, but he felt as it were a cold breath float from her and envelope him. He saw that she had perceived his incredulity and resented it with contempt. He felt his anger rise. They left the table ere he had recovered his equanimity ; and the Duchess taking possession of Edith, carried her off to set her at ease with the younger members of the party.

She was received by Miss Tellinghurst, a

handsome, heavy-looking girl, with a stiffness that seemed habitual to her ; and by Lady Sophia Bentwell, a slender, sallow brunette, who presented a general likeness to a sparrow, with voluble affability. She told Edith she was delighted that she had come, and said that she had often heard of her; an assertion which reposed on the solitary fact of the Duchess having announced her expected arrival, and Ormanby Averil having been heard to say that she would be the beauty of the coming season.

Miss Tellinghurst soon retired to her room to write letters, the afternoon proving so stormy as to render walking, driving, or riding, impracticable ; and Lady Sophia ensconced herself in a recess with Edith, and devoted herself to amusing her.

" I suppose you don't know all the people here," she said, turning her quick glance down the spacious room, with its scattered groups.

" I know none of them," replied Edith.

" Except Ormanby Averil ; I heard him say

he knew you; and Lord Skeffington;—I wonder where he is, by-the-way. Oh, I remember, he'll be back for dinner."

" I know Lord Skeffington slightly. I scarcely know Mr. Averil at all."

" However, he's the best worth knowing of them all—perfectly delightful when he chooses. Don't you find him so?"

There was an almost imperceptible upward motion to Edith's eyebrows, as she answered,

" I have only seen him once before to-day."

Lady Sophia caught the momentary expression. It impressed her profoundly.—Here was some one that did not care for Ormanby Averil!

" May I ask you to tell me the name of the lady in the dark blue moire; the duke is speaking to her. I did not catch it."

" Oh, the lady who was talking with you before dinner. That is Madame Wosocki. She's immensely clever and accomplished, and very good-natured. It's quite delightful to see the way in which she treats her husband. There he is in the furthest window, wiping his spectacles."

" What, that little old man! He looks old enough to be her grandfather."

" So he is,—old enough, I mean. She was married to him at sixteen, and they seem very fond of each other. You never saw anything so splendid as her diamonds. That tall woman with black eyes is Lady Masterton. They say she worried her daughter-in-law to death. I don't know about it : but one thing is certain, and that is that her son won't speak to her. She is talking to Lady Melby; isn't she sweet, with her brown hair, and eyes just of the same colour, and that lovely smile. She is a cousin of Ormanby Averil's, and l'amie intime of the Duchess. That stiff, sensible-looking woman crocheting lace is Lady Emmeline Horsmantle. Nobody would imagine it to see her sitting there so quietly, but she is a perfect heroine. She has done such things! She went with the General when the troops marched against the Sikhs."

" Oh yes," said Edith, " I read of it in the papers. Is that really she?"

She gazed eagerly on the plain, quiet, rather sad-looking lady in a black silk dress and simple collar, who was so intent upon her delicate work. " How sad she looks."

" I don't think she has anything to make her unhappy, I mean now-a-days. She had a great deal of trouble when she was young."

" And where is the General?"

" There he is, that oldish man, with great black eyebrows and white hair, talking to Frank Westwood at the end of the room; he looks as if he were lecturing him. Frank is his ward, and is always getting into scrapes. That pale young man, with sandy hair and a great forehead, is Lord Prudhoe. He is immensely clever and rich; but so bookish, that every one is afraid of him. He writes reviews, and cares for nothing but sanitary reforms, and poor-houses, and all that sort of thing. His mother is very pious, as they call it. She put all that into his head. It's a great pity."

And Lady Sophia's eye rested disapprovingly on the young man who would have been such an unexceptionable parti, had it not been for his oddity. Edith looked at him also, but with a very different expression. Lord Prudhoe, as people always do when they are looked at, turned his glance suddenly towards the two girls. He averted it almost instantly, but not before he had perceived Edith's sympathetic look. He was not used to appreciation. He did not expect it. He knew that, despite his silence and reserve, he was looked upon with an evil eye, and stigmatized as a radical by all his own set. He felt keenly the isolation in which his heretical convictions had placed him; yet was too manly and conscientious to swerve one iota from his allegiance to what he considered political truth, no matter how painful the forfeiture he thereby incurred. And so the earnest look of approbation which he had seen on

Edith's face gave to him a novel delight. Again and again it recurred to him.—What could have caused it? Lady Sophia could not have been saying any good of him. She was gazing at him at the same moment with an unmistakable expression of reprobation on her sharp little face. What could it have been?—And so powerful a magnet did his mingled curiosity and admiration prove, that when Ormanby Averil returned from the stables where he had been to inspect a recent purchase of the Duke's, he found Lord Prudhoe deep in conversation with Edith. He took up a review, seated himself in shadow, and watched them unobserved over the top of the pamphlet. Lord Prudhoe's usually stiff and reticent demeanour had changed. He was talking earnestly—to judge by the countenance of his listener—eloquently. For Edith possessed that rare and peculiarly feminine power of drawing out, as it is called, those who conversed with her.

"I am very glad I took your advice," said the Duchess, coming up behind Averil's chair. "She is really an exquisite creature, too pale you would say of anyone else, yet it seems to suit her style. And she must be clever; look at Prudhoe, how interested he seems. I never saw him talk that way to any one before; and whatever his faults may be, lack of brains can't be counted among them. I wish he would marry a quiet, amiable girl like that, and settle down rationally."

The Duchess moved away and left Averil to his review.

The day began to darken; the rain, which had pattered unceasingly upon the window panes, fell faster and faster; the ruddy glow of the fire triumphed over the paler illumination of the fading daylight. Work was folded up, and books laid aside; the guests drew nearer the fire in a general causerie, preparatory to the anticipated summons of the dressing bell; still Averil sat watching; still Lord Prudhoe talked on, quite unconscious of the lapse of time, and still! Edith listened.

When the dressing bell rang, Lord Prudhoe's habitual reserve rushed back upon him.

"I must beg your pardon," he said, looking much disconcerted. "I had no idea I had been talking so long. You must excuse me. I fear I have been boring you."

"Not at all. I have enjoyed it extremely."

Edith raised her eyes to his disturbed countenance with one of her rare smiles. Averil, looking up, saw the radiance which for a moment overspread her face, fully revealed by the firelight, and saw it with a thrill of jealous anger.

"Conceited coxcomb!" he muttered between his teeth, glancing at Lord Prudhoe; and drawing his tall figure to its fullest height, he went up to dress for dinner in a mood which did not tend towards his valet's peace of mind.

His place at the dinner table was nearly opposite Edith, who was seated between young Westwood and the General. Lord Prudhoe was at a safe distance, taking his soup with his customary grave countenance, and replying at times, apparently much against his will, to Lady Sophia's incessant rattle. No danger that Prudhoe should engage

in any conversation. He was disposed of for the
next two hours at least. Solitude, temporary
though it had been, had brought counsel to Mr.
Averil. He proceeded with judgment. For the
first half-hour he did not open his lips. He left
Edith's attention to be claimed by Frank Westwood, a dandy of the first water, as inane and
affected as befitted his pretensions. He noted
the increasing silence and reticence with which
Edith met his advances; he marked the growing
look of ennui on her face; and when he perceived
that she was thoroughly *dégouté* with her neigh-
bour, then, and not till then, did Mr. Averil
skilfully engage the General in conversation, and
by means of adroitly putting questions, and art-
fully expressed uncertainty, enticed the unsus-
pecting veteran into a detailed and graphic
account of some of the most interesting episodes
in the Indian wars. Edith's face roused from its
look of listlessness; her eye, which had hitherto
avoided his, at length rested on Averil's face as
he plied the general with his apt queries. At

length, as if reading Edith's wishes, Averil spoke of Lady Emmeline. Here the General grew less communicative—·he obviously did not like to bring before others those traits which rendered his wife so dear to him; but Averil's respectful attitude, and Edith's imploring look overcame his first reluctance, and he recounted, with glistening eye, the story of her courage, her endurance, her self-devotion, and tireless exertions, in all that time of danger and distress.

With such tact did Averil manage and prolong the conversation, that it lasted until the Duchess gave the signal for retiring. He had gained his point. Edith had been pleased and interested, if not by him, at least through him. "Give me but time," said Averil to himself, as he watched her retiring figure. "I never yet tried to please a woman in vain." And Ormanby Averil drank his sherry and dissected his nuts, and thought what a beautiful creature Edith Arden was.

"What do you find to talk about with Prudhoe?" asked Lady Sophia, seating herself on a bergère near Edith, as the ladies spread themselves through the drawing-room; "I can't imagine. I think him so stupid. He tires me to death."

Edith suppressed a half smile, inspired by the doubt on which of the two, Lady Sophia or Lord Prudhoe, the burden of weariness had pressed the more grievously.

"I did not find it necessary to talk much. I preferred to listen."

" Did he not bore you."

" Not at all. I found him very pleasant."

" Really? How strange! I can't understand it at all."

And Lady Sophia shook her head incredulously.

" What is it that Lady Sophia cannot understand?" asked Princess Wosocki, coming forward " May one inquire?"

" I was saying I did not understand Lord Prudhoe; but he is one of your favourites, I believe."

"Yes ; I like him much, though I cannot agree with him at all. He was born too soon or too late. He does not belong to the world as it is," she added, turning to Edith.

Lady Sophia took advantage of the movement to effect her retreat. With all her admiration of Madame Wosocki, she never dared talk to her, being haunted by an uneasy suspicion that the Russian was looking through her all the time.

"You would ask me why," continued the Princess, taking her place beside Edith. "Is it not so?"

Edith smiled.

"It is because he believes too much. He has made an Utopia, as you call it—an ideal; and he would hurry on the world to that. The world is not ready. It must have time."

"But would the world ever advance were it not for such men as he?"

"I think it would. The march of an army does not depend upon that of its vanguard."

"But are not reformers the sappers and

miners, rather, of that great moving mass?" asked Edith, looking up earnestly. "Do they not make straight and easy the ways which would else be hard to tread? do they not hew down forests, and bridge over rivers, and make that progress possible, which, for lack of them, might else come to a stand-still? Can the world do without such men?"

"Do not think that because I do not agree, I cannot sympathize," said Madame Wosocki, "but here comes Lady Masterton."

Lady Masterton, in her imposing amplitude of crimson velvet, her haughty head thrown back, its every feature inflated by habitual pride, her hard, defiant eyes seeming to smite all they looked upon, swept towards them.

"We were just discussing one of your compatriots," said Madame Wosocki, moving so as to make room for Lady Masterton on the sofa, "Lord Prudhoe."

Lady Masterton fanned herself vindictively.

"Prudhoe is a conceited, meddling fool," she

said, harshly. " If he and those like him had their way, they would make a red republic of us at once. It is bad enough when tailors, and shoemakers, and weavers, get their heads turned with talking their own abominable trash, but when it comes to a gentleman's wanting to level everything, and throw away everything that's worth having, I think he ought to lose his position. I had a great mind not to come when I heard he was to be here," and she glared angrily around. " But I wanted to ask the Duchess something, there she is."

Lady Masterton, still fanning herself, as if to keep down the combustion of her indignation, swept away.

"That is what Lord Prudhoe has to meet in his own class. He is a man born to disappointment. I am sorry for him, for I like him much."

She rose as if to break off the conversation, and seating herself at the piano-forte, began to run her fingers over the keys. Her eye roved at random over the room a-while, then rested on

Edith, as she sat near the foot of the instrument, her face turned from the groups beyond. Every sound ceased through the room, every ear was inclined to catch the notes. It was seldom that the princess played. The Russian's look grew deep and grave, as she gazed on the countenance before her, her touch more searching, more powerful. The instrument sighed and moaned inarticulately under her fingers for a few moments in a plaintive prelude, then the scattered notes of its recitative gathered and formed themselves into the harmony and rythm of a low, soft chant. Into its modulations stole the whisper of running brooks, the rustling of leafy boughs, the trills and warblings of the spring-time birds, while still the chant kept on, full and deep, its tender burden mingling with the woven brilliancy above. A murmur of delight broke from the listeners, but as silence again stilled around the song, a wild plaint as from afar broke across its happy measure, gradually coming nearer and nearer, until the sunny gladness was drowned in the slow and solemn echoes of a dirge for the dead.

Edith's eyes had rested as if fascinated upon the Russian's. She sat spell-bound, fixed to the spot, while that mysterious music translated and sent back on her ear the secret anguish within her. She longed to rise and flee, but she could not move. She must stay and listen to it all.

As the music ended, the peculiar look left the Princess's eyes. It was replaced by an expression of regret, almost of remorse. She left the piano-forte, and seated herself by Edith's side.

" Forgive me," Edith thought she heard her whisper, but when, in her uncertainty, she glanced at her companion, she saw Madame Wosocki's eyes fixed upon the carpet, her lips pressed firmly together as though no word had passed them. She did not perceive Ormanby Averil, who had left the dining-room before the rest, and who, leaning in the shade of the great curtain of the doorway, had been watching them both. He left his post, unnoticed, spoke a few words to Lady

Melby, then advanced to where Edith and Madame Wosocki were seated, still in silence.

" Will you not play something else ?" he asked; "something to quiet the pain such music gives ?"

Madame Wosocki looked at him an instant, then rose and resumed her place at the pianoforte. He seated himself on the sofa, at a little distance from Edith.

" I cannot bear to hear such music," he said, as if half to himself.

She glanced at him. He was looking down. His face was grave and overshadowed. He said no more.

As the polonaises and mazurkas succeeded each other with their capricious changes, the tension of Edith's nerves relaxed. When the music ceased she had regained all her self-command.

" How pleasant it is to hear music like that once in a while," said Averil. " One gets so horribly tired of such music as one usually hears, that you're tempted to believe that you never cared for anything of the sort; when, all at once you meet with something like this, and you find out that it isn't music that you've been vilifying, but only a base imitation."

" I don't know much about what music one usually hears," replied Edith; " but I am glad to know that I shall not often listen to such as Madame Wosocki's."

" I'm half tempted to agree with you, not with regard to the music, but to the place. Music so penetrating and suggestive as that should not be listened to, except when we're free to follow out the train of thought it suggests."

" I don't know whether that would always be an advantage."

" Perhaps not. There was something very sinister about that first piece. It might be called the ' Song of Life.' "

" Are all lives so sad? I should be sorry to think so."

" Yes; there isn't any such thing as a happy life. It doesn't exist. Men and women say they are happy from pride, because they don't want anybody to pity them; but what miserable wretches they are *au fond*. I don't know a soul I'd change with, and—" He stopped; his expression filled out the sentence—" I'm not particularly happy myself."

" I cannot quite believe that," said Edith. " I can't think that so much misery can exist, except it be deserved, and certainly every one doesn't deserve to be miserable."

" Possibly not. There's Madame Wosocki herself, for instance. It certainly wasn't her fault that the man she was to have married was killed in a duel a week before the wedding day. But, nevertheless, she has been consistently miserable about it ever since."

" How could she have married, then?" Edith asked.

Averil looked at her as if he found her very naïve.

" I suppose she thought she did enough to prove her constancy in choosing a man of seventy.

Her being miserable doesn't interfere with her seeming very contented, as you see; and as Lady Sophia, whom I saw talking to you industriously after lunch, has probably already informed you, her diamonds are magnificent."

Edith looked up quickly.

" No, I didn't hear her," continued Averil, smiling drily; "but it's not difficult to predict the run of Lady Sophia's conversation. She gave you an account of the people here; it was rather superficial, but, on the whole, not illnatured."

" Yes; she seems amiable," said Edith.

Averil had expected that his reference to Lady Sophia's shallowness would have met with some response, yet he was pleased that Edith allowed it to pass unnoticed. He looked at her, and wondered what she was thinking in her mind.

Edith turned a glance upon Madame Wosocki.

" Shall I give you the true mot d'énigme of Madame Wosocki's marriage?" he asked, in a different tone from that he had first used in speaking of the subject.

" I wish you would," she said earnestly.

" Her parents gave her the choice of three lovers, after a suitable time; and she took the one for whose character she had the greatest esteem. It's very simple, you see. The Prince is the most attentive of husbands, and she gets on very well with him, in spite of her early troubles."

" How dreadful to live in such a country," Edith said slowly, after a pause.

" Where daughters can't say no, you mean. It isn't quite the thing we're accustomed to in novels; but in real life it seems to answer very well. And besides, as to that, matters go on pretty much the same in England as anywhere else."

Averil brought his sentence abruptly to a close as he looked at Edith's unconscious face. He wasn't particularly sensitive, but he shrank from indulging his habitual vein of irony. He couldn't talk to her as he did to other people. There was something about her that rebuked his customary caustic vein.

" But certainly English fathers are not like those on the Continent," replied Edith, look-somewhat perplexed.

" Certainly not," responded Averil, acquiescently. " In all the foreign plays I ever saw, the good fathers were invariably drawn on the English model."

He glanced at Mr. John Arden, and mentally calculated how much disinterestedness would enter into his plans for the final disposition of his daughter.

" Then they were probably caricatures," returned Edith. " I don't think it possible for a foreigner to comprehend English character. They have no conception of what lies deepest in it."

" And what is that? may I ask."

" The love of truth," Edith answered, fixing her eyes upon him.

Averil winced internally. He did not feel particularly truthful himself at that moment. He would turn the conversation back to the plays.

" I can't say they came very near the proto-
type, for the most part. The foreign idea of a
bon père de famille is usually bald, very fleshy,
and has a tendency to redness of the face;
whereas with us the highest embodiment of the
paternal principle is rather tall, has a slight
stoop in the shoulders, and benign blue eyes, set
in a somewhat pale face, of great delicacy of
outline and refinement of expression. I'm not
sure that I quote correctly, but that's the style,
isn't it? There's an essential difference, you see."

" I perceive," replied Edith. " It's Mr.
Caxton, as opposed to the butler."

" Just that. They're capable of the butler;
but Mr. Caxton is as completely out of the range
of their intellectual vision as if he were the first
of the Pharaohs."

Averil was interrupted by the entrance of the
gentlemen. Lord Skeffington, who had come in
too late to speak to Edith before dinner, and who
had been seated at a distance from her at the
table, came towards her.

"So you have really come. I didn't half believe you would. I'm immensely glad, I am, indeed."

Edith expressed her pleasure at again meeting Lord Skeffington, who forthwith took the place which Averil vacated much against his will.

"It's alarmingly quiet, though, you know," continued Lord Skeffington. "The Duchess's brother, whom she detested, died last month, and we're all invited down here to grieve for him. We can't dance because of the lacerated state of our feelings, and we can't act charades or anything of that sort, because we are overpowered by our grief. We're a little more cheerful now, but when I first came down all the dogs had weepers on, and a puppy was solemnly turned off the estate one day and left to starve on the high road, because in an access of unfeeling gaiety he had torn off his crape. I don't know when I've been so impressed. You should have seen the dinner table that day; everyone spoke in whispers."

"I am glad that the general key is a little

raised," replied Edith, smiling. "I'm afraid it might have had serious consequences had it continued as you describe it."

"Oh, but the serious effects were produced, I assure you. I began to write a serious poem, "Beyond Despair." Rather striking, the title, don't you think so? I began it to keep my spirits up. Everything goes by contrast, you know, and it was quite cheerful and exhilarating compared to the company in the drawing-room. But as I said, things are a little better now ; we have begun to return to our normal condition."

"There is a lady who seems to have remained in a rather stern mood," said Edith, glancing at Lady Masterton, who upon seeing Lord Skeffington take his place near Miss Arden, had raised her eye-glass and deliberately examined her, inclining to consider the girl in the light of an enemy, because her awful scrutiny had caused no sign of embarrassment.

Lord Skeffington turned his eyes in the direction of the glance which had accompanied Edith's remark.

"Remain—well, yes, perhaps remain is the word, for there's no chance of her getting out of it. They say that she struck out right and left as soon as she was born, and she has never stopped that exercise up to the present moment. She is a dreadful woman, quite dreadful. Lady Sophia, there by the window, talking to those black whiskers, she's her daughter you know."

Edith made a sign of assent.

"You see how thin she is; that comes of Lady Masterton's having kept her on bread and water so much. People say that for everything she did when she was a child she was put on bread and water, and I believe it, for I've watched her, and she hasn't touched bread nor tasted water since she has been here. Fortunately some one died, and left her a pretty fortune in her own right not long ago, and she has grown quite brisk since then, for Lady Masterton changed her tactics at once, and began to call her 'dear Sophia.'"

"Really you are quite scandalous," said Edith, laughing. "Are you not afraid of the return of all your idle words upon you? What an army they would make."

"I've nothing to be afraid of there," replied Lord Skeffington, gravely; "nothing at all. What would become of society if it didn't have its truth tellers. I am one of the world's censors, that's all."

"In that case you are never in want of occupation."

"Never. I'm the busiest man alive. I'm writing my memoirs, to be published two hundred years after my death. I fancy that by that time I shall be dust, so that I can't be exhumed and burnt by the descendants of my contemporaries."

"What nonsense are you talking now to Miss Arden?" said the Duchess, coming up, somewhat to Edith's relief, for she didn't quite like the turn the conversation was taking.

"I was talking of literature, your Grace," replied Lord Skeffington, demurely ; and the Duchess, after a few words to Edith, moved away, stopping a little further on to speak to Miss Tellinghurst.

From memoirs, Lord Skeffington diverged to various of the guests, concerning whom he communicated much extraordinary information, all of which Edith found diverting, and a small portion of which she believed.

Meantime Averil had retired to the other side of the room, where the Princess was sitting alone.

She glanced up as he approached, and motioned him to a seat beside her. She looked depressed.

" You are tired," he said, fixing his eyes upon her.

" Yes, a little."

" You have been reading."

There was a certain meaning in his tone.

" *Comment ?*"

" I saw you."

She slowly made a sign of assent.

" What did you discover ?"

She flashed a look at him.

" That I shall not say."

" Then you discovered a secret."

" Every woman is a secret."

" But if you were sure I should make no bad use of the knowledge ?"

She turned her eyes scrutinizingly upon him.

" I am in earnest," he said, bending forward. " I do not ask from simple curiosity."

" I see it," she said.

" And you will not trust me ?"

" I have no right. I know nothing. What are you asking ?" she answered, in an impassive tone.

" You are playing with me. I ask a very simple thing, that you will give me your impressions of a new character."

" Because that new character interests you."

" Precisely."

" Very well, then I tell you one thing—I will not help you."

" What do you wish to say ?"

"I mean that you are not a person to bring peace or happiness to any young girl, and I will not say one word, nor reach out one finger, to help you."

" Pardon me ! I think you must have misunderstood me," said Averil, stiffly.

Madame Wosocki smiled a peculiar smile—penetrating, keen.

" Ah, do not take the trouble to say things to evade. You know that I only speak when I am sure. Do you think I cannot see ?"

" See what ?"

" *Que vous êtes amoureux de cette jeune fille.*"

The blood rushed to Averil's face.

" Granted I were," he replied, after a pause, " what should you then say ?"

His voice vibrated nervously as he spoke.

" Mon ami, I do not think she will ever marry you."

" Why ?"

" Are you in earnest? Shall I really tell you? Will you not be angry ?"

" No.   Speak."

The Princess turned and looked at Edith where she was standing by a shaded lamp, whose subdued reflections played over her dress, and made a sort of moonlight around her.

" All her wishes are aspirations ; she tends upward.   She craves the beautiful, the good, the noble.   Could you make such a woman as that happy were she your wife ?"

Averil's face darkened.

" I do not say that you are worse than other men ; I think, on the contrary, that many men are worse than you ; but I ask you fairly, are you worthy of that young girl ?"

Averil made no reply.

" You may think I am bizarre and extravagant. —I am not.   I see every day young women who marry riches, and titles, and place, and I say to myself, it is very well. They are educated for that ; it will make them happy.   But when I see a nature such as I see there, I say—It is not for these that she must marry ; she must have more."

" What must she have ?"

" She needs a heart unstained, a soul the home of noble thoughts, a mind broad, clear, and deep, fit to develope and expand her own. She needs love, such love as men feel before they have learnt to make a lie of truth and a jest of sin. And so I say again I will not help you; I will not tell you what I read just now. I will not put into your hand the key to her thoughts."

The Princess's eyes flashed, and her nostrils spread. A look of determination settled over her face. Her resolution was obviously one not to be altered.

" I see I cannot hope that you will be my friend," he said. " Promise me, at least, that you will not be my enemy."

There was no anger in his voice. He was too politic for that. He must not have Madame Wosocki for his opponent.

" Promise me at least that," he reiterated.

" You have thought only of her ; think a little

what this might be to me.   It might make a different man of me."

The Russian looked down a few moments
thoughtfully before she spoke. She said at
last,

" I feel I am doing wrong, yet I promise.
Don't thank me."

She rose abruptly and joined a group at a little
distance.

—" *Vou vêtes amoureux de cette jéune fille.*" Was
he really at length in love ? he who had thought
his every possibility of loving had been destroyed
long ago, had withered out of existence, when he
had stood by that bedside, had heard that faint
voice murmur, " Don't be afraid to tell me ; if
you knew how glad I am to die ;" and had seen
those gentle eyes close on the life he had blighted,
close too soon to allow him to offer the one *insufficient* reparation.—He lived it all over again
as he sat in the solitude of the peopled drawing-
room. Again he stood by that white tombstone, again

he read the accusing words, " Clara, wife of the Hon. Henry Hilesday, aged twenty years." Again he turned his face from that grave; but this time not as then, not with that hard, bitter grief, that seemed to poison all he looked on, that remorse which had refused to be forgotten, or stifled, or crushed, that had haunted him for thirteen years, dogging his footsteps, whispering at his shoulder, obtruding itself when most unwelcome, never so distant but that one moment could summon it before him. To-night that ghost of memory seemed laid, sleeping with Clara in her far-off grave beside the Adriatic.—But he could not sit there dreaming all the evening. He must rouse himself and do as others were doing;—and he talked with Prince Wosocki and the Duchess, and listened to a French romance, shrill and sentimental, from Lady Sophia; and to an English ballad, monotonous and pathetic, from Lady Melby, and learnt from Mr. John Arden how timid Edith was on horseback, and won a look of gratitude from her by offering to drive her with Lady Melby in a pony carriage the next day; and burnt three letters in a woman's handwriting, letters of no very distant date, when he went upstairs that night.

And Edith lay in the ancient chamber and listened to the hollow murmur of the waves, and drew in a patient courage from the sound;—the time would come when all pain would be over,—and she fell asleep in dreamless slumber, unwitting how closely her fate was pressing upon her unconscious steps.

CHAPTER VIII.

EDITH could never clearly recollect how the first days of her visit at Albansea had passed. Her outer and inner consciousness were so at variance as to give her, at times, a distressing sense of unreality. The remembrance of her misery lay like a leaden weight upon her, and yet she must dress, and speak, and listen, and smile through it all, as if she were happy, as if nothing had happened, as if Walter loved her still.

Lord Prudhoe, Madame Wosocki, Mr. Averil, Lady Melby, and Lord Skeffington were those she liked best to talk to. Mr. Averil was never cold or disagreeable now. He was kind, and attentive, and entertaining. He

never tired her.　Lord Prudhoe was very nice.
She had a great respect for him; but he seemed,
she did not exactly know, perhaps she was mistaken, but she feared he was beginning to care
a little too much about talking with her.　She
preferred to talk with Mr. Averil, and Lord
Skeffington, who was always amusing.　Madame
Wosocki was delightful; Edith felt as if she had
known her all her life; and Lady Melby was
very gentle and lovely.　She often talked with
Edith.　She seemed to have a great liking and
esteem for Mr. Averil.　She had told Edith of
many kind deeds that he had done, such things
as one would never have dreamed of coming
from such a man, and all calculated to raise
Ormanby Averil in her esteem.　Every man does,
as it were perforce, a certain amount of good in
his life, and all that Averil had ever accomplished
was in these conversations duly chronicled by his
cousin. She had spoken of him once to Edith as a
person much to be pitied.　What could it have
meant?

It meant that Mr. Averil had been far too prudent a man to attempt to play single-handed the game he had undertaken. He knew the world too well not to be fully aware of the necessity of an ally, and an able one. He would have preferred the Princess for his advocate could he have engaged her, but as it was, neutrality was all he could hope from her. Lady Melby could serve his aims almost as well, however, and Lady Melby he would lose no time in securing. Accordingly, on the second evening of Edith's visit, after circling through the various groups and making himself universally agreeable, he at length approached his cousin.

" I have come here to rest," he said, casting himself indolently beside her. " I have been on duty for two hours."

" I have seen and admired you. Really you made yourself as pleasant as if you had not been Ormanby Averil," replied Lady Melby, from whom Averil was in the habit of hearing *ses vérités.*   And to his credit be it spoken, he never took offence at her plain speaking.

"So I am a monster in general, am I?" he answered, settling himself comfortably in the corner of the sofa.

"Something of that sort."

"Monsters have many different characteristics; would you humanely inform me which are mine?"

"You know them as well as I do. Why should you ask?"—Lady Melby was too much a woman of the world to attempt to reform anyone.

"But should I tell you that I wish to get rid of them?"

Lady Melby replaced in its saucer the tea cup she was on the point of raising to her lips, and gazed at Averil in amazement.

"I shouldn't believe you," she replied after a pause.   "But you won't say so."

And she drank the tea and gave him the cup to set down on the console beside him.

" You think me an insufferable egotist."

What could he be aiming at?

" Precisely."

Averil's tone of levity changed.

" Do you remember what made me so ?"

Lady Melby gave an imperceptible start. He had never, friends and cousins though they were, never before referred in her hearing to that chapter of his past.

" Blame me," he continued, " blame circumstance, fate, anything you will, but don't think that what I am is what I wished to have been ?"

" You are not old, Ormanby, you are but in the prime of life. Why say wished to have been ?"

" What is there that could change me now ?" he answered moodily.

She looked at him wistfully. She was fond of him. She had always regretted the aimless life he led. She thought him capable of something far better. She wished, yet hardly dared to speak.

"Speak,—that is if you have anything to say."

"My answer would only be what every one who has dared has said to you for the last ten years."

"You mean to say that I should marry?"

"Yes, Ormanby, that is what I mean."

"Perhaps you would be so good as to go a step further and give me your advice as to the choice of a wife," he said with something of his usual sarcastic inflection.

Lady Melby drew back.

"You cannot think I would be so rash."

"Then you are willing to see me caught up by some adventuress in her teens, married for money, prospective rank and position. Thank you, I prefer my existence as it is,"

"Is there no alternative between such a marriage and no marriage at all?"

"What girl do you know that would not weigh these in the balance before she rejected me with them for some other man without them? Can you mention one?"

" There are scores, I have no doubt."

" Then you can easily bring them up to refute me."

Lady Melby hesitated ; it was not quite so easy to think of scores of totally disinterested young ladies.

" There would be no use in naming them, you wouldn't believe me."

" Do you think Lady Sophia would accept me if I were to offer myself to her this hour?"

" Yes, I suppose she would."

" Or Miss Tellinghurst?"

" Probably."

" Do you think Miss Arden would ?"

Averil could not succeed in rendering his tone quite as unembarrassed as he desired, but Lady Melby did not perceive the change.

" That is more doubtful," she replied. " She impresses me differently from other girls."

" And you think that a man of thirty-five cannot hope to win the affection of a girl of seventeen."

"Not at all. That is not what I meant."

"What is it then?"

"I don't think that she would marry except from strong personal preference, and I do not believe she would feel that preference for anyone who was not in love with her."

"But if I tell you that I am in earnest?"

Lady Melby looked eagerly in his face.

From that moment her active co-operation was secured.

CHAPTER IX.

"THAT is a pretty stamp," Edith remarked, as the letters which fell to her father's share in the division of the contents of the post-bag, passed her on their way up the breakfast table. "What is it?"

"That's Greece, " replied Lord Skeffington who was seated next her. "It's touching to see such candour on the part of a government, isn't it? They've chosen the head of the god of cheats and liars as a device, you see."

"Immensely profitable affair the loan that Greek house is negotiating just now," said Lord Masterton, a little higher up the table. "If I were a capitalist, I think I should engage in it largely. I see it was taken up at once."

" It promises well," answered Mr. Arden, somewhat constrainedly ; and he betook himself to sorting his letters.

" What a heavy letter," exclaimed Lady Sophia, passing along the line a voluminous package, directed to Mr. Averil, the last of the general distribution. " Anyone would say that a poor author had sent you a manuscript."

Averil glanced at the post-mark, then carelessly tore open the envelope.

" It is from Houston Lacy," he said. " It gives an account of the theatricals, I see. But why should she sign herself Mrs. Williams ?"

" That was to be her character in the play," said Edith, who had been kept informed by Isabel of every detail.

" I wish she would apply, and stop this advertisement," remarked the Duke, who was unfolding the "Times." " I am tired of seeing it. It is the first thing that meets my eye every morning when I open the paper ; " and he read aloud,—

" Mrs. Williams, recently residing at No. 35, Chadlink Street, is earnestly requested to apply at the office of Pettyman and Kelson, 40, Bulton Street, where she will hear of something greatly to her advantage."

" I knew a Mrs. Williams once," said the General, meditatively, plunging his spoon into an egg ; " but that was in India, let me see, nearly twenty years ago.　It can't be she."

" Was she a pretty woman, General, that you remember her so long?" asked Lord Melby, a fresh-complexioned, round-faced man, with droll eyes and grey whiskers.　" She must have made an impression on you; and you were a bachelor then, if I am not mistaken."

" Right in one thing, wrong in another," responded the General, good-naturedly.　" I was a bachelor; but she wasn't a pretty woman, chaplains' wives never are—it's a curious fact.　However, that puts me in mind that she had with her, under her care, as you might say, the handsomest woman I ever saw, the wife of Captain—Captain—'pon my word, I forget his name,—a fine young fellow he was, too."

" How came she to be under anybody's care if she were married?" enquired Lady Sophia, whose pleasantest anticipation connected with matrimony was that of complete and sovereign independence.

" She was learning to speak English, for she was a Frenchwoman, I believe. It was a hill post, and I could look from my verandah across to theirs. She seemed a quiet, modest, silent young woman enough. No one to have looked at her would have guessed what she was."

" And what was she? Anything queer about her?" asked Lord Melby, helping himself to a muffin.

" Faith, I scarcely know myself. All I can say is that troubles suddenly broke out in the hill country, and we received marching orders. All the women were sent to a place of safety, except this Mrs. —, I forget her name; but she refused to stir. She insisted upon marching with us, and she went. 'Pon my soul, I believe she was the devil. The first skirmish we had I saw her in the hottest of it. Her eyes were all in a blaze. I shouldn't have known her but for her dress. She seemed to revel in it, and it was brisk work,—they were five to one of us. She killed three natives that day with her own hand. One of them had struck down her husband. She galloped up just in time, put her pistol to the fellow's ear as he had his arm up, and blew his brains out. I saw it. 'Pon my word, I believe I was afraid of her, and the men were afraid of her, too. I couldn't believe my eyes when I saw her the next day, riding along as quiet and still as if she had never smelt gunpowder."

" What a dreadful woman!" exclaimed Lady Sophia. " I wish I could have seen her."

" At a safe distance," suggested Mr. Averil. " Not quite the person one would like to meet tête-à-tête. Do you feel any draught, Miss

Arden ?" he asked, as Edith shivered. " But, General, one is inclined to fancy a person possessed of the pleasing characteristics you mention, as rather of the hag order, grisly and grim. Are you quite sure she was so young and handsome ?"

" I never saw anyone so handsome in my life," stoutly asseverated the general. " And her husband doated on her. Though she could be such a tigress on occasion, she was as gentle and submissive to him as a slave."

" I say, General, you seem to have devoted a good deal of time to studying that household," said Lord Melby, laughing. " Wasn't the young captain jealous of you ? "

" He hadn't any cause to be," returned the General. " I never exchanged a word with the woman in my life. It was an odd thing, she never would speak to anyone except her husband and Williams and his wife."

"How very odd ! What a pity you can't remember her name. Where did she come from ? " asked

Lady Sophia, whose curiosity, always simmering, had now reached boiling point.

"'Pon my word, I can't tell. I knew once, but it is so long ago that I have forgotten. All I am sure of is that she was the handsomest woman I ever saw," replied the General, whose memory seemed but indifferently good on all minor points, though sufficiently clear on what he evidently considered the main one—the exceeding beauty of the Captain's wife.

Edith had listened with breathless attention. Could the name have been Hartley? She longed to ask, but an inexplicable reluctance held her silent. She did not dare to identify this beautiful Amazon with the person to whom her presumptions pointed. She shuddered at the idea of having pressed so recently that blood-stained hand. She could not think of it. She would drive it from her mind. She wished she had been at the other end of the table so as not to have heard the conversation.

She was standing idly by the window an hour

later, trying to interest herself in the gambols of some black and tan terriers, which, in a state of ecstatic delight from some cause unknown, were exhibiting their gymnastic accomplishments on the gravelled walk that skirted the empty moat, when Mr. Averil came towards her with a letter in his hand.

Averil had carefully studied Edith's character during the days they had been together. The easy intercourse among the guests which naturally resulted from the smallness of the Duchess's circle had offered him opportunities by which he had sedulously profited; while at the same time he had strictly avoided making his attentions so marked as to put her on her guard. He had beheld with carefully concealed delight the departure of Lord Prudhoe, who had suddenly disappeared the morning after a conversation with Edith in the conservatory ; and Averil had even carried his diplomacy so far as to praise that young man in Edith's hearing, and to wonder what could have caused his abrupt leave-taking, thereby inexpressibly relieving her mind, and convincing her that she was the only person of the circle who had any idea of the circumstances which had brought about his defection. She enjoyed ta king with Mr. Averil. She was sorry when he would leave her to chat with Lady Sophia or Mrs. Tellinghurst, but he seemed to like to talk with them as well as he did with her.

Averil studiously maintained this impression in Edith's mind. He had made his approaches cautiously, feeling his way, making sure of each step. He saw that he must exert every best faculty he possessed in order to win her ; and the task of so doing was not difficult. With her he felt himself a different man. His passion for her heightened his powers, refined his sentiment, and sharpened his mental sensations, blunted as they had become through long contact with the world. He grew young again while conversing with her. All the glow and ardour of past years came back, through her he lived again. But all was not soft in the feelings she inspired. The thought of failure thrilled him with fierce pain. He resolutely averted his eyes from the possibility of a rejection.—He must, he would succeed.—And as he said it his brow lowered heavily, and his look grew cruel in its intensity. There was more passion than tenderness in Ormanby Averil's composition.

But as he now approached Edith with the open letter hanging from his hand, all traces of these stormy midnight reveries had fled. His forehead was unruffled, and his look breathed only that calm composure which gave him so great an ascendancy over those with whom he associated. Nor was this the result of any violent effort on his part. By some apparent contradiction, Edith's presence had the power of quieting the emotion that the thought of her raised within him when absent. There was something so delicate, so pure, so noble, in the young girl's nature as to for the time exalt and refine every sentiment of those who approached her. And so it was that Ormanby Averil found himself living two separate existences, as the higher and the lower powers of his mental constitution alternately held him under their sway.

She looked up as he came near.

" Do I interrupt you ?" he asked.

" Not at all.   I was only watching the dogs," she answered; " and I don't find it very interesting," turning from the window.

" Then perhaps you may feel inclined to hear a part of this letter. It gives quite a detailed account of the amusements at the Park."

Edith would very much have preferred not to have heard the letter, but what reason could she give for refusing? She must say that she should be very glad. And she said so, and seated herself in the deep embrasure of the window where she could turn away her head and watch the clouds, while Averil drew a chair near her and arranged the sheets in order.

" You have reason to be alarmed," he said, as he completed the task, " but I beg that you will stop me as soon as you begin to feel tired. Mrs.

Lacy is not often so prolix, but, as I judge from the aggressive style of her opening, she was in remarkably high spirits at the time."

"Please don't skip the first," said Edith, as she perceived him about to lay down the first sheet. " I should like to hear, that is if you are willing."

In fact she felt some little curiosity to know how anyone managed to be aggressive, as he termed it, to so very dignified a person as Mr. Averil.

He glanced at her, uncertain whether to consent. A momentary gleam of girlish mirthfulness played over Edith's face as she caught the glance. It arched her pensive lips, danced in her large, deep eyes, and seemed to ripple in the soft gold of her hair. It was a new expression to him, bewitching, inexpressibly alluring. He bent his head over the paper to hide the flush that rose to his cheek, the quick fervour that glowed in his eye, but instead of reading as she requested, selected another page.

"I think this passage about Miss Hartley would be more interesting to you," he said. "She had to act unexpectedly, it seems." He began to read—

"I never saw anything so lovely as she looked. Lady Tremyss and her maid had hunted up some old dress. It was of stiff white silk embroidered in silver. There hadn't been time to powder her hair, but it had been raised a little, and covered with a Marie Stuart cap of point d'Angleterre, and round her neck she wore Lady Tremyss' splendid row of pearls.

"We all crowded round her, admiring and complimenting her, but she did not seem to care for a word we said. She only asked Arden if that would do, and when he said yes, she went and sat down by herself. I do wonder why they try to make a secret of that engagement. Isn't Arden there all the time?"

Miss Tellinghurst came up at this moment.

"We are going in twenty minutes. Had you not better put on your habit?" she said.

"I will read it later," said Averil, rising as Edith rose.

A few days earlier Averil would not have thought of reading this letter to Edith, but he had now insensibly placed himself upon a footing that he felt emboldened to try the effect of this half confidence.   He had made use of the knowledge he had gained of her character to attack her on her most undefended side.   He had approached her through her father.   Her own perception of his deficiencies had rendered her painfully sensitive as to the estimation in which he was held by others.   This Averil soon discovered and turned to account.   With his own peculiar tact he chose every occasion of bringing out Mr. Arden in conversation.   He payed respectful attention to his every utterance, and by the authority of his opinion reinforced that of Edith's father on all disputed points.

Mr. John Arden's native abilities and great

accuracy of special information, joined to that keenness of apprehension and command of language which belong to men whose mental powers are habitually kept in a state of activity, rendered it no difficult thing to Averil to accomplish what he had undertaken—the raising John Arden in the estimation of the guests at Albansea. The effect on Edith was all that he could have hoped. Thence gentle looks and friendly converse, and rare radiant smiles, reaped by Averil; delicious rewards, but all insufficient, as he felt, with growing passion, day by day. He longed with impatience that he could scarcely curb, to break down the barrier of sweet reserve that shut him out from all nearer approach. He felt the reticence imposed upon him by their mutual position all but intolerable. He had never been thwarted in his life. Satisfaction had followed so closely on his every wish as to leave him a prey to satiety. Patience and self-control had in no wise entered into his plan of life. His cold and composed demeanour at once concealed and indicated indomitable will.   And now that the hours were so rapidly passing that were to be the last of Edith's stay, he felt the impulse to risk a declaration to be almost uncontrollable. Hence it was that he had sought the opportunity of reading to her his sister's confidential missive, hoping to feel his way through Edith's reception of it to a still closer advance.

Sir Francis Lester came towards Edith as she reached the door.

"Now, Miss Arden, don't forget that your father has promised for you.   It's very fine now, but I think it will cloud up later.   We shall just have time for the ride, I fancy."

"I hope I shall have a gentle horse," said Edith, "I am not a good horsewoman."

She mounted the great staircase and proceeded to the antique chamber where Félicie stood busily brushing and arranging the riding habit and small plumed hat.

Meantime Averil took himself to the stables, and carefully selected the easiest saddle and the gentlest horse. This accomplished, he sought out Mr. John Arden, whom he found writing letters in his room, important letters, if one were to judge by the absorbed expression of his face. The interview was brief. The two men shook hands as they parted.

" At any rate she will be safe," said Mr. Arden, after a long pause.

" Ah, me voilà enfin contente," exclaimed Félicie, as she moved dexterously about the room. " Mademoiselle va monter à cheval Mademoiselle sera coiffée à ravir avec ce petit chapeau de chez Liégault. Moi je n'aime pas voir les demoiselles coiffée en homme : passe pour Mademoiselle Teeleenyurst, et pour l'autre ; mais pour Mademoiselle, ça ne lui ira pas du tout."

And chattering volubly, Félicie proceeded to dress Edith in the closely fitting habit, carefully knotted up the curls under her hat, and buttoned on the dainty little boots.

" Mon Dieu," she ejaculated, as Edith turned

to leave the room, " Mademoiselle ne va pas
sortie toute habillée en noir ! Si Mademoiselle
veut seulement attendre un petit instant que je
lui mette une petite cravate bleue.   Il y en a une
bien étroite.   Où est elle donc ?"

And she began hastily to search for the needed
touch of colour.

" Come, Edith, everyone is waiting," said Mr.
Arden's voice at the door.

Edith, escaping from Félicie's hands, ran
down stairs, her heart cheered by the affectionate
embrace and kiss her father bestowed upon her as
she left her room.

" Mais c'est en deuil qu 'elle va sortir,—quelle
triste présage.   Je n'aime pas ça du tout, moi,"
said Félicie, looking at the door through which
Edith had vanished ; and she shook her head
ominously as she went to the window and tried
to catch a glimpse of the cortége.

The party proceeded much in the order that
Averil had anticipated, and ere long Lady Sophia
and Miss Tellinghurst, with their respective cava-

liers, were out of sight. Sir Francis would gladly have remained near Edith, but his horse was restive, and fretted the other horses so much as to visibly distress her; for though a graceful she was not an expert horsewoman. Accordingly Sir Francis executed himself, as our French neighbours say, and dashed forward to regain the rest of the party.

"Where are we going?" asked Edith, as they turned into a narrow path which seemed to lead directly to the foot of a steep and wooded hill, gay and green doubtless in summer time, but now sad and dismal enough.

"We are going to the ruins of Merliton. They are not much in themselves, but they command a fine view of the sea and the plain between."

They made their way up the precipitous path which led to the crest of the hill, Averil leading Edith's horse by the bridle. Passing through a broken archway, they entered upon a plateau of narrow extent, bounded by ivy-grown masses of crumbling stone. Beneath them stretched far and wide a brown and withered plain; beyond rolled the surges of the sea. The sky, fair in the morning, was becoming overcast. Clouds were gathering in the distance. A hollow sough wailed from the distance, ominous of an approaching storm.

"We have moralized and sentimentalized until we are quite blue, while we have been waiting for you," said Lady Sophia, as Edith and her companion appeared. "You have no idea what you have lost."

"Then are we to have none of the benefits of those moralizings and sentimentalizings?" asked Averil with a provoking smile; he wanted her to go. "Are you going to leave us to our feeble resources? Certainly you will not be so uncharitable. Pray take compassion on us and favour us with a repetition."

Miss Tellinghurst giggled, Sir Francis looked awkward, Westwood and Prynne exchanged smiles, and Lady Sophia turned red. The moralizing and sentimentalizing had consisted in a brisk discussion of the respective merits of the horses ridden by Lady Sophia and Sir Francis, and an exchange of bets as to which would first reach a certain heap of stones some half mile distant.

"I won't stay to be made fun of," she exclaimed with an embarrassed laugh, "I shall take advantage of what is left of fine weather for a gallop."

Leading her party she took her way down the path. The sound of the clattering, slipping, and scraping of the horse's hoofs and the echo of the voices of their riders gradually sank in the distance, and Edith and Averil were left on the plateau alone.

For a time neither spoke. Edith's eyes were fixed on the heaving ocean and on the darkening sky. As Averil glanced at her he saw an inscrutable expression on her face. Her lips began silently to move. What could it be that sent its shadow outward from her mind, and drew so strange a veil of hidden meaning over her face?

"Do not think me presumptuous, I beg," he said, in his gentlest tone; "but may I ask you, as they ask in the old game, what your thought is like?"

"I was repeating to myself some lines."

"May I hear them?"

"They would not please you."

"Independently of any poetical merit, I should like to hear them."

Edith reluctantly complied.

> "Thou gentle one,
> God's mystic messenger,
> When, 'gainst the sinking sun,
> On some glad hill top, shall I see thy feet?
>
> "Where tarryest thou?
> Above what silent couch
> Bend'st thou thy shadowy brow?
> To what sad ear speak'st thou His message sweet?
>
> "Into what caves
> Of dreamless sleep dost thou,
> Far from Life's storm tost waves,
> Lead the expectant ghost thou summonest?
>
> "Look where I stand,
> And wait. Oh, Death, come near,
> Stretch forth thy misty hand
> And lead my soul into those halls of rest."

As she spoke, Edith's voice grew fuller and

deeper; a smile of mournful exultation settled on her face. Never had Averil felt himself so over-mastered by her peculiar beauty as now that he saw it illumined with that mysterious smile. Never had he felt himself so madly in love with her as now.

He spoke. His words came with difficulty.

"Not only death, life also may be called a Silent Land," he said. "How many of us dare not speak our deepest wishes, our dearest hopes, but keep silence until silence becomes too hard to bear."

Edith turned her eyes upon him with a bewildered, half-terrified look.

"This morning I have spoken to your father; and it is with his full consent that I come to ask you if you will become the angel of a hitherto worthless life; if you will aid me to be what I ought to be; if you will save me from pain and disappointment that I dare not think of; if you will make me at length worthy to gain your affection."

Edith sat with pale and parted lips.

Mr. Averil loved her. Her father wanted her to marry him. She could not marry him. She did not love him. Averil read it all on her face. He changed his ground.

" I do not ask for any response save the liberty to try to make myself acceptable. Our acquaintance has been too short to give me any hope of having gained your preference. I do not ask for a promise, a pledge of any sort. I only ask to be received as a suitor whom you remain at liberty to reject at will."

He paused and fixed a look, intent, burning, upon her.

" I am more sorry, more grieved than I can say," she said. " But I should be doing wrong, —I cannot—I must not offer you any encouragement. I never thought of it before, but I feel it impossible."

Her voice grew stronger as she proceeded. There was no maiden timidity, no concealed gladness, no restrained triumph to be read upon

her face. It was full of sad and grave concern—
nothing more. Averil was silent. The volcano
within him gave forth no sign.

" Forget this," she said kindly, almost affec-
tionately. " I, too, will forget it. Let it be
between us as if it had never been. Will you not
promise me that ? "

And she held out towards him her gloved hand.
Averil took it, and bowed his face over it, and in
calm, measured words promised as she requested,
and in his heart the same instant swore an oath
that, willing or unwilling, Edith should be his
wife.

All that was good in the man went to the
ground before this shock of disappointment, was
engulfed in this shipwreck of his hopes. Within
him was but a seething hell of jealous rage and
passion. The savage who has his den in the
heart of every one of us, rose triumphant within
the high-bred gentleman, astute, cruel, vindictive,
violent ; all the more dangerous because concealed
from sight. Averil gazed upon her ; he noted

every girlish charm, and said to himself, " All this shall be mine ; " while Edith, grateful to him for the quiet self-command with which he had listened to her rejection of his suit, and for his abstinence from all outpouring of regret, congratulated herself that though she could not care for him in the way he wished, she had yet secured him as a friend.

Madame Wosocki met them in the hall as they came in. She saw Averil's face, more sallow than usual, all the lines harder, the eyes filled with pale light; and marked the friendly glance Edith threw him as she turned to ascend the staircase. It was enough.

" He has proposed and been rejected. Now I may speak—and I will."

She followed Edith upstairs and overtook her in the gallery. She placed her hand on the girl's arm.

" Beware of that man," she said, in a low voice.

" What man ? " returned Edith, surprised and startled.

" Ormanby Averil."

And Princess Wara vanished into her own room.

As Edith entered her chamber, she saw not Félicie, but the tall figure of her father. She was taken in his arms and pressed warmly to his heart.

" My pet, my dear child, I am truly happy," exclaimed Mr. Arden, kissing her with overflowing affection.

Edith's heart sank at the sight of his beaming face. It would be a great disappointment to him. She had not known that he cared so much for it. Even had she known, it could not have altered anything.

" But, Papa," she began timidly, " you do not know—"

" Yes, my dear, I know. I saw Mr. Averil this morning. Just what I should have wanted for you. Everything that could be desired, and one of the best titles in England in prospect."

" But, Papa, I have refused him," she uttered reluctantly.

Mr. Arden looked stunned.

"Refused him!" he repeated mechanically, then with sudden and angry vehemence, he exclaimed, "Is the girl crazy!"

"Papa, Papa, don't look so," pleaded Edith. "I don't care for him in that way. I could not."

"Care for him in what way? Is there anything against him? One of the best matches in England. And all out of sheer folly!" burst from Mr. Arden's lips as he stalked the room with agitated strides. In fact he had not once contemplated the possibility of Edith's rejecting such an offer. He was utterly unprepared for this check to his ambition. He was exasperated, and like most men when angry, somewhat brutal.

Edith stood like a guilty creature in the middle of the room. Her father had never been angry with her before, and she was bewildered by this sudden outbreak of indignation. She could not at the moment collect her thoughts to reason upon it. She only felt a confused sense that she must have done something very wrong, else her father would never have spoken in such a way to her.

"And pray what reason did you give to Mr. Averil," asked Mr. Arden, confronting her.

"I said I could not give him any encouragement."

"You seem to have forgotten that you have been giving him encouragement ever since you came here."

"Oh, Papa!"

"Have you not treated him with marked pre ference? Have you not always shown yourself ready and willing to talk with him when you would scarcely speak a word to other men? You have drawn him on, and now you throw him over in this way. Most unworthy treatment for a gentleman of his claims."

"Papa!"

"Don't speak to me in that way as if I were ill-using you, when I am merely telling you the truth. You have not the right, no girl has the right to trifle so with any man, especially of such a position."

"But, Papa, you would not have me marry him if I don't love him," she said imploringly.

"And what is there to prevent your loving him?"

She made no answer.

"Do you want to marry any one else?"

"No, no!" she exclaimed hurriedly.

"Then why should refuse him leave to pay his addresses?   How do you know whether you can love him or not until you have tried?"

"I feel I could not," she answered in a low but steady tone.

"Feeling has nothing to do with it.   Marriage is a serious thing; a great deal beside feeling is involved in it.   I tell you, Edith," he broke out with increasing vehemence, "that you don't know what you are doing; you don't know of what importance this marriage may be to you."

He walked hastily about the room, then stopped before her.

" I shall tell Mr. Averil that he must not take your refusal as a final one, that you were quite unprepared, and need time for deliberation."

" But, Papa, thinking of it will make no difference. I couldn't marry him ; I couldn't."

She looked beseechingly in her father's face, but it was closed against her. John Arden only saw menaced ruin on one side, and on the other Edith's hand blindly pushing away the support that would save herself, that might uphold him from totally sinking in the gulf below.

" Edith, this is no time for folly. I have told you what I shall do, and I shall do it. If you have any sense of duty you will not oppose me. I know of more than you do."

Mr. Arden left the room as Félicie knocked to say that her young lady would have but just time to get ready for luncheon.

Edith changed her dress and descended to the apartment below, where the other guests were already assembled, where at the same moment she was to meet Mr. Averil and her father.

Could it really be that she had treated Mr. Averil ill? If he had thought so, surely he would not have so frankly accepted her offered hand, and promised that they should always be friends. And yet her father seemed so sure!

She shrank into a seat in the most retired part of the room, behind a table, and bent her head over some books which lay upon it.

"Let me show you these. You will find them more interesting. They have just come down," said Averil's voice beside her, as he laid before her some water-colour drawings.

She glanced up gratefully. His tone was as quiet and unembarrassed as if nothing had passed betwixt them; but her look sank back perplexed from its momentary scrutiny of his face. There was a change, subtle, almost imperceptible, but a change which filled her with undefined uneasiness. The eyes looked on her as from a stranger's face; the lips seemed rigid as they moved, remarking and commenting with ready fluency on the separate beauties of each sheet he turned over.　She could not tell how, but it was as if, though present, he had suddenly been removed to an immeasurable distance from her.　His body was there, but no soul seemed to inhabit it.　The link between Edith's mind and his was broken ; it had snapped at the moment of his silent, obdurate oath.

After lunch Averil disappeared, nor could Mr. John Arden find him any where.　At dinner he was peculiarly affable to the banker, near whom he was seated, but as soon as the gentlemen returned to the drawing-room he engaged in a game of whist, which lasted till bed-time.　If any further advances were to be made, they must come from Edith's father.　It did not suit Averil's policy to show any eagerness.　And the next morning, after breakfast, Mr. Arden, fulfilling Averil's expectation, requested the favour of a few words with him in Mr. Arden's own room, in the course of half an hour.　Then the banker retired to read his letters while awaiting Averil's appearance.

But when Averil, punctual to the appointment, knocked at the door, no voice from within replied. It was strange. His own apartment was on that side of the house. He had heard Mr. Arden enter his room, and he was certain that he had not left it again. He knocked a second time— no answer. He turned the handle of the door and entered.

Prone on the hearth-rug lay Mr. Arden, his right hand resting on the fender. As Averil bent over him he saw a paper close to the fire, yellowed and scorched by the heat. He took it up and ran his eyes over its contents. It was a despatch, principally written in cypher. There were several names, Greek and Turkish, contained in it, which the writer had apparently not thought it necessary to disguise.

Averil placed the paper in his breast pocket, then rang the bell violently.

The news spread quickly through the castle. In a few moments Edith, pale and speechless, was kneeling beside the bed, holding her father's unconscious hand, apparently deaf to the consolation and encouragement offered by the Duke and Lady Melby, who had closely followed her ; the Duchess' feelings were too keen to allow of her presence.

Mr. Averil maintained his station in the sick room. As he leaned over the mantel-piece and fixed his eyes upon the fire from which he had just snatched the secret which had stricken down its owner, a look strangely out of accordance with the scene gleamed over his face, a look of cruel, crafty self-gratulation.

After a space, long as it seemed to Edith, but of whose duration Averil had taken no heed, the physician who had been summoned in all haste, *en attendant* till Sir Joseph Slingsby's arrival, was announced and Lady Melby came to Edith's side.

" Excuse me, but the physician is here. It would be better that you should leave the room for a few moments, my dear Miss Arden."

She rose obediently to her feet.

" I want to see the doctor afterwards."

" You shall do so.   Now may I take you to
your room?"

Edith glanced around.   Her eyes rested on
Averil.   He read their mute entreaty, and came
forward.

" I will not leave him an instant," he said.

She looked her thanks, and left the chamber
as Dr. Winter entered.

He was a tall, stooping, middle-agd man, with
mild, undecided features.   He advanced, bowing
respectfully to the Duke and Averil ; turned an
uncertain look upon Wilson, apparently not sure
whether he ought to bow to him or not, but by a
happy inspiration decided in the negative ; then
began his examination of the patient.

—The case was simple enough, and he was happy
to say did not present any very alarming symp-
tom.   The pressure on the brain did not appear
extreme, and would probably be immediately re-
lieved by bleeding.   He did not approve of bleeding in general, but there were some cases where
it was advisable, it might indeed be called strictly

necessary, and this seemed to him to be one of them.—

The vein was opened. The blood dropped slowly at first, so slowly that Averil frowned, while Dr. Winter fidgeted nervously with the lancet. At length the current flowed more freely, Mr. Arden half opened his eyes, groaned, shut them again, then opened them widely and stared about the room.

"Don't be disturbed," said the Duke, placing his face near that of the sick man. "You have had a fainting fit, but all is right now."

Mr. Arden did not seem to understand what was said to him, but the Duke's steady tone and look appeared to compose him; he closed his eyes and remained quiet.

"I'll go and tell the Duchess that he's better now," said the Duke in a low voice to Averil. And he left the room.

The physician watched silently by his patient until the colour of his face paled to something like its natural hue; then he quitted the bedside,

and Mr. Averil sent Wilson with a cheering message to Edith. When they were left alone he drew
Dr. Winter to the window.

"This must have had a cause," he said, in a low
and somewhat confidential tone.

"Most certainly, most certainly," responded
Dr. Winter.

"Such seizure as this may originate in several
different things, I presume."

"Yes, indubitably."

"May I ask what you should consider most
likely to have brought on such an attack ? "

There was something exceedingly soothing and
persuasive in Averil's voice, yet Dr. Winter, unaccountably enough, felt somewhat uneasy as he
met the gaze of the sick man's friend.

" I should be inclined to mention too full habit,
or some sudden shock, as the most probable
cause."

" Yet Mr. Arden is not plethoric."

" No, he does not appear so ; certainly not."

" In that case, since you reject plethora, you

feel obliged to attribute it to some mental emotion of a painful character."

Averil's eyes gleamed like steel, as he fixed them on Dr. Winter's face.

" I think that plethora is not admissible under the circumstances ; certainly not,"said Dr. Winter, turning his gaze upon the well-built and in no wise corpulent figure of his patient. " I think I must rather incline to some sudden strain upon the mental faculties; but even there I may be mistaken. It is difficult to pronounce at first sight clearly upon such a case. It is necessary to have some knowledge of the attendant circumstances, in order to decide ; and here that knowledge is necessarily wanting, as I have not had the honour of any previous acquaintance with my distinguished patient."

" Perhaps, in the strictest confidence, and simply to afford you some hint that may be of use in your treatment of the case, I ought to say that Mr. Arden is, in fact, suffering under the influence of a very painful occurrence."

" Of recent date? No remote distress would be capable,—you understand; that is to say, it is not probable."

" The event to which I refer is but a few hours old; in fact, it was in order to converse with him upon it that I came in just now, when I found him insensible."

" I think that settles the question," replied Dr. Winter, nervously turning from the gaze of his interlocutor. " At least it appears to me to do so, quite."

" It might then be well, since such is your opinion, to state it to Miss Arden," said Averil, in his most courteous tones; " it would tend to lessen her anxiety; only I should prefer that you should not mention our having spoken on the subject together, as it might be disagreeable to her,—you understand."

Dr. Winter did not understand at all; but, as Averil seemed to expect that he should say he did so, he assented. And accordingly, in his interview with Edith, he informed her that he must state it as his opinion that the origin of her father's seizure was not to be attributed to any state of repletion of the arterial system, but rather to some sudden and violent action on the brain. He assured her that all danger for the moment was over, and that he hoped his distinguished patient would soon be in his usual state of health. And rather uncomfortably impressed by Edith's pallid silence, Dr. Winter bowed himself out.

" Some sudden and violent action on the brain—some sudden and violent action on the brain—" The whole air seemed filled with voices, repeating the words. Edith sank down, and rested her face on the chair whence she had risen at Doctor Winter's entrance. She could not think, she could not reason, she could but listen to those accusing voices repeating the physician's words.

It was an hour later when Averil, sitting in Mr. Arden's room, saw a white figure with fixed eye and blanched lips, glide into the chamber.

Edith seemed walking in her sleep. She stood an instant by the bedside, then going to the table gathered up the letters and papers which were lying there, placed them in her father's desk, and bore it away. As she reached the door she turned and cast a searching glance around, as if to assure herself that nothing had escaped her; her eye passed over Averil as if she did not perceive him, then she left the room.

Edith opened and read every letter, examined every document.

The possibility had suggested itself to her that some disastrous business complication might have caused her father's seizure; but she could discover nothing that gave any colour of probability to the surmise.

After she had read and laid aside the last paper, she sat for a while motionless, then drawing towards her her portfolio, she wrote a few lines to Mr. Tileson, her father's confidential clerk. In them she communicated the fact of her father's alarming seizure, and urgently requested him to inform her whether there were anything in the position of his affairs which could have been its cause. This done, she returned to her father's room.

The mental work she had been through had roused her energies. She had rallied from the first shock. She would not look forward, she would not look back; she would think only of what was to be done hour by hour. The answer to her letter would arrive the next day, till then nothing was to be gained by thinking where every ground of conjecture was so uncertain.

So Edith tended her father all that day; sitting at the foot of the bed, her eyes fixed upon his face all the time that she was not more actively employed. There was little, however, to be done. Mr. Arden scarcely spoke; he groaned from time to time; but when Edith asked him if he were in pain he answered no.

Mr. Averil had left his post when Edith came to assume her station in her father's room; but each hour of the day he came to the door to learn from Wilson of his master's state.

The day passed, passed with that stealthy fleetness which the sense of danger always brings with it.　In the evening the physician so anxiously expected arrived; but, after seeing him, Edith felt that she knew nothing more of her father's state than she had done before.　She could extract nothing from him, except indefinite assurances as to Mr. Arden, and positive charges as to not over-fatiguing herself.

And Edith, according to his orders, went to her room, drank the cup of tea which Félicie had ready for her, lay down still dressed, and tried to sleep.

She had just completed her toilette on the next morning, when there came a light tap at the door.

" Madame la Duchesse," Félicie announced, and the Duchess came in with a letter in her hand.　She stayed but for a few moments, only long enough to express her sorrow and sympathy, then left Edith to the perusal of the letter.

Mr. Tileson, in old-fashioned phrase through whose formality appeared his very sincere distress, lamented Mr. Arden's illness, and then proceeded to assure Edith that there was nothing whatever in the state of the house to have given its head the slightest uneasiness. On the contrary, its affairs had never been so prosperous, and the important foreign negotiations recently undertaken, he would state in confidence, and only completely to reassure Miss Arden, promised to double the very large capital invested in them. He concluded with renewed regrets.

There are moments when we seem to have drank the cup of suffering dry,—when from the pangs of our mortal anguish is born a courage which fills us with its own unnatural strength, and drives us forward to action on whose consequences we dare not look ;— moments when the soul sweats blood, when it sends up, through the midnight of its despair, its cry of agony ; and when, that supplication unanswered, it rises and goes forth, still, uncomplaining, resolved, to its crucifixion.

And such moments were those that Edith spent in the twilight of that hushed and shadowy room, sitting beside the curtained bed whereon lay stretched her father, watching and waiting for him to awaken from the slumber into which he had sunk.

At length Mr. Arden's eyes unclosed. They rested on his daughter's face. He sighed, and turned them away.

Edith rose. Her very flesh shrank and quivered as she bent over him and said,—

" Papa, only get well, and I will never oppose you any more."

END OF VOL. II.

T. C. Newby, 30, Welbeck Street, Cavendish Square, London.

BEDSTEADS, BEDDING, AND BED ROOM FURNITURE.

HEAL & SON'S

Show Rooms contain a large assortment of Brass Bedsteads, suitable both for home use and for Tropical Climates.

Handsome Iron Bedsteads, with Brass Mountings, and elegantly Japanned.

Plain Iron Bedsteads for Servants.

Every description of Woodstead, in Mahogany, Birch, and Walnut Tree Woods, Polished Deal and Japanned, all fitted with Bedding and Furnitures complete.

Also, every description of Bed Room Furniture, consisting of Wardrobes, Chests of Drawers, Washstands, Tables, Chairs, Sofas, Couches, and every article for the complete furnishing of a Bed Room.

AN

ILLUSTRATED CATALOGUE,

Containing Designs and Prices of 150 articles of Bed Room Furniture, as well as of 100 Bedsteads, and Prices of every description of Bedding

Sent Free by Post.

HEAL & SON,

BEDSTEAD, BEDDING,

AND

BED ROOM FURNITURE MANUFACTURERS

196, TOTTENHAM COURT ROAD,

LONDON. W.

WILSON'S
PATENT DRAWING-ROOM
BAGATELLE AND BILLIARD TABLES,
WITH REVERSIBLE TOPS.
Circular, Oblong, Oval, and other Shapes, in various Sizes
FORMING A HANDSOME TABLE.

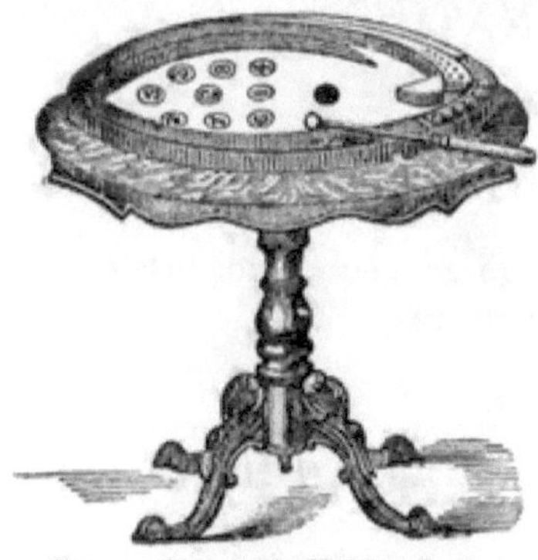 

Patent Bagatelle Table--Open.   Patent Bagatelle Table--Closed.

Prices from 5 to 25 Guineas.   Prospectus Free by post.

WILSON AND CO., PATENTEES,
Cabinet Makers, Upholsterers, House Agents, Undertakers, &c.,
18, WIGMORE STREET (Corner of Welbeck Street), LONDON, W.; also at the
MANUFACTURING COURT, CRYSTAL PALACE, SYDENHAM.

In 1 Vol. Price 12s.

ON CHANGE OF CLIMATE,
A GUIDE FOR TRAVELLERS IN PURSUIT OF HEALTH.
By THOMAS MORE MADDEN, M.D., M.R.C.S. Eng.

Illustrative of the Advantages of the various localities resorted to by Invalids, for the cure or alleviation of chronic diseases, especially consumption. With Observations on Climate, and its Influences on Health and Disease, the result of extensive personal experience of many Southern Climes.

SPAIN, PORTUGAL, ALGERIA, MOROCCO, FRANCE, ITALY, THE MEDITERRANEAN ISLANDS, EGYPT, &c.

" Dr. Madden has been to most of the places he describes, and his book contains the advantage of a guide, with the personal experience of a traveller. To persons who have determined that they ought to have change of climate, we can recommend Dr. Madden as a guide."
—*Athenæum.*

" It contains much valuable information respecting various favorite places of resort, and is evidently the work of a well-informed physician."—*Lancet.*

" Dr. Madden's book deserves confidence—a most accurate and excellent work."—*Dublin Medical Review.*

TEETH WITHOUT PAIN AND WITHOUT SPRINGS.

OSTEO EIDON FOR ARTIFICIAL TEETH,
EQUAL TO NATURE.

Complete Sets £4 4s., £7 7s,, £10 10s., £15 15s., and £21.

SINGLE TEETH AND PARTIAL SETS AT PROPORTIONATELY
MODERATE CHARGES.

A PERFECT FIT GUARANTEED.

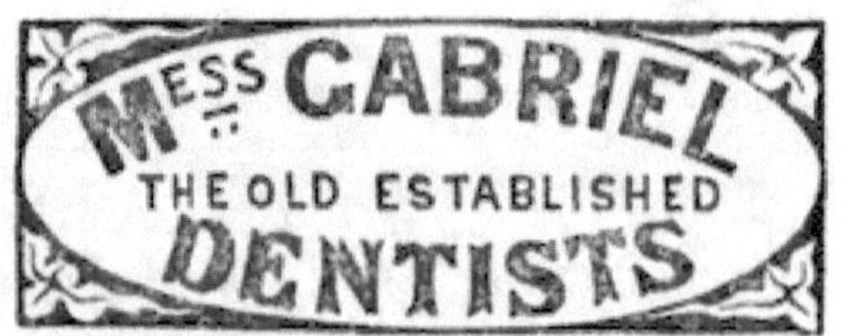

London:

27, HARLEY STREET, CAVENDISH SQUARE, W.
134, DUKE STREET, LIVERPOOL.
65, NEW STREET, BIRMINGHAM.

CITY ADDRESS :

64, LUDGATE HILL, 64.

(4 doors from the Railway Bridge).

ONLY ONE VISIT REQUIRED FROM COUNTRY PATIENTS.

Gabriel's Treatise on the Teeth, explaining their patented mode
of supplying Teeth without Springs or Wires, may be had gratis
on application, or free by post.

THE TOILET.—A due attention to the gifts and graces of the person, and a becoming preservation of the advantages of nature, are of more value and importance with reference to our health and well-being, than many parties are inclined to suppose. Several of the most attractive portions of the human frame are delicate and fragile, in proportion as they are graceful and pleasing; and the due conservation of them is intimately associated with our health and comfort. The hair, for example, from the delicacy of its growth and texture, and its evident sympathy with the emotions of the mind; the skin, with its intimate relation to the most vital of our organs, as those of respiration, circulation and digestion, together with the delicacy and susceptibility of its own texture; and the teeth, also, from their peculiar structure, formed as they are, of bone or dentine, and cased with a fibrous investment of enamel; these admirable and highly essential portions of our frames, are all to be regarded not merely as objects of external beauty and display, but as having an intimate relation to our health, and the due discharge of the vital functions. The care of them ought never to be entrusted to ignorant or unskilful hands; and it is highly satisfactory to point out as protectors of these vital portions of our frame the preparations which have emanated from the laboratories of the Messrs. Rowlands, their unrivalled Macassar for the hair, their Kalydor for improving and beautifying the complexion, and their Odonto for the teeth and gums.

THE

GENERAL FURNISHING

AND

UPHOLSTERY COMPANY

(LIMITED),

F. J. ACRES, MANAGER,

24 and 25, Baker Street, W.

———

The Company are now Exhibiting all the most approved Novelties
of the Season in

CARPETS, CHINTZES,

MUSLIN CURTAINS,

And every variety of textile fabric for Upholstery purposes
constituting the most recherché selection in the trade.

J. W. BENSON,

WATCH AND CLOCK MAKER, BY WARRANT OF APPOINTMENT, TO
H.R.H. THE PRINCE OF WALES,

Maker of the Great Clock for the Exhibition, 1862, and of the Chronograph Dial, by which was timed "The Derby" of 1862, 1863, and 1864. Prize Medallist, Class XXXIII., and Honourable Mention, Class XV, begs respectfully to invite the attention of the nobility, gentry, and public to his establishment at

33 & 34, LUDGATE HILL,

Which, having recently been increased in size by the incorporation of the two houses in the rear, is now the most extensive and richly stocked in London. In

THE WATCH DEPARTMENT

Will be found every description of Pocket Horological Machine, from the most expensive instruments of precision to the working man's substantial time-keeper. The stock comprises Watches, with every kind of case, gold and silver, plain, engine-turned, engraved, enamelled, chased, and jewelled, and with dials of enamel, silver, or gold, either neatly ornamented or richly embellished.

BENSON'S WATCHES.

"The movements are of the finest quality which the art of horology is at present capable of producing."—*Illustrated London News* 8th Nov., 1862.
33 & 34, LUDGATE HILL, London.

BENSON'S WATCHES.

Adapted for every class, climate, and country. Wholesale and retail from 20 guineas to 2½ guineas each.
33 & 34, LUDGATE HILL, London

BENSON'S WATCHES.

Chronometer, duplex, lever, horizontal, repeating, centre seconds, keyless, astronomical, reversible, chronograph, blind men's, Indian, presentation, and railway, to suit all classes.
33 & 34, LUDGATE HILL, London.

BENSON'S WATCHES.

London-made levers, gold from £10 10s., silver from £5 5s.
33 & 34, LUDGATE HILL, London.

BENSON'S WATCHES.

Swiss watches of guaranteed quality, gold from £5 5s ; silver from £2 12s. 6d.
33 & 34, LUDGATE HILL, London.

Benson's Exact Watch.

Gold from £30 ; silver from £4.
33 & 34, LUDGATE HILL, London.

Benson's Indian Watch.

Gold, £23 ; silver, £11 11s.
33 & 34, LUDGATE HILL, London.

BENSON'S CLOCKS.

"The clocks and watches were objects of great attraction, and well repaid the trouble of an inspection."—*Illustrated London News*, 8th November, 1862.
33 & 34, LUDGATE HILL, London.

BENSON'S CLOCKS.

Suitable for the dining and drawing rooms, library, bedroom, hall, staircase, bracket, carriage, skeleton, chime, musical, night, astronomical, regulator, shop, warehouse, office, counting house, &c.,
33 & 34, LUDGATE HILL, London.

BENSON'S CLOCKS.

Drawing room clocks, richly gilt, and ornamented with fine enamels from the imperial manufactories of Sèvres, from £200 to £2 2s.
33 & 34, LUDGATE HILL, London.

BENSON'S CLOCKS,

For the dining room, in every shape, style, and variety of bronze—red, green, copper, Florentine, &c. A thousand can be selected from, from 100 guineas to 2 guineas.
33 & 34, LUDGATE HILL, London.

BENSON'S CLOCKS,

In the following marbles :— Black, rouge antique, Sienne, d'Egypte, rouge vert, malachite, white, rosée, serpentine, Brocatelle, porphyry, green griotte, d'Ecosse, alabaster, lapis lazuli Algerian onyx, Californian.
38 & 34, LUDGATE HILL, London.

THE HOUSE-CLOCK DEPARTMENT,

For whose more convenient accommodation J. W. BENSON has opened spacious show rooms at Ludgate Hill, will be found to contain the largest and most varied stock of Clocks of every description, in gilt, bronze, marbles, porcelain, and woods of the choicest kinds.

In this department is also included a very fine collection of
BRONZES D'ART,

BENSON'S ILLUSTRATED PAMPHLET, free by post for three stamps, contains a short history of Horology, with prices and patterns of every description of watch and clock, and enables those who live in any part of the world to select a watch, and have it sent safe by post.

33 & 34, LUDGATE HILL, E.C.